10682827

ONE WAY OUT

London financier Morgan Dale is travelling by train to Scotland with his chief clerk, Martin Lee. Suddenly he's confronted by the woman who'd been obsessed by him — his ex-secretary Janice Elton. Dale had recently sacked her and spurned her romantic advances, but now she wants revenge. However, when Lee returns to their carriage, he finds Janice's dead body and Dale claiming she'd committed suicide by taking strychnine. Soon there will be only one way out for Dale . . .

JOHN RUSSELL FEARN
and PHILIP HARBOTTLE

ONE WAY OUT

Complete and Unabridged

LINFORD
Leicester

First published in Great Britain

First Linford Edition
published 2013

British Library CIP Data

Fearn, John Russell, 1908 – 1960.
One way out. - - (Linford mystery library)
1. Detective and mystery stories.
2. Large type books.
I. Title II. Series III. Harbottle, Philip.
823.9'14–dc23

ISBN 978–1–4448–1473–6

Published by
F. A. Thorpe (Publishing)
Anstey, Leicestershire

Set by Words & Graphics Ltd.
Anstey, Leicestershire
Printed and bound in Great Britain by
T. J. International Ltd., Padstow, Cornwall

This book is printed on acid-free paper

1

Death on a Train

A cloud of smoke, a deluge of sparks, and a roar like a hundred Niagaras — then screaming onwards into the winter dark, rocking over the points, blasting through remote and solitary stations, gradually coming ever nearer towards Scotland. The Scots Express was two and a half minutes behind time, and the passengers within it were well aware of the fact as they swayed gracefully with the lurching of the train.

Morgan Dale, London financier, muttered something uncomplimentary as he dropped his ballpoint and rocked back from the sheet of calculations he was studying. Instantly his chief clerk dived to retrieve it. He held it out in a thin hand.

'Thanks,' Dale growled.

'He seems to be making up for lost time, Mr. Dale,' the chief clerk murmured, but this time he only received a grunt in reply. Morgan Dale had gone back to his calculations, his broad back wedged into the upholstery of the corner seat as he strove to keep himself steady . . .

The two men had the first class reserved compartment to themselves and the blinds were drawn — save one, which gave a limited view of the corridor outside. Beyond it there was a vision of shifting lights in the darkness as towns and homesteads fled by. Martin Lee, the chief clerk, sat looking at the lights through his own reflection, his thoughts miles away. He was a rather weary-looking man of average height, neatly dressed, with a thin pale face and emaciated hands.

He was a very capable chief clerk, otherwise he would not have kept his job with Morgan Dale for over twenty years. He was also a good mathematician and, though few would have suspected it, a deep schemer. And he hated Morgan Dale absolutely. He loathed the man's dominance, his monetary power, and his apparent mastery of every difficult situation . . . Deep in the mind of Martin Lee was an insatiable longing to change places with Morgan Dale — not physically, of course, but circumstantially, and make *him* take the orders for a change.

Martin Lee sighed over the vain speculation. That had always been the trouble throughout his life: he had always dreamed vast dreams, and never seen them materialise. Indeed he had made no particular effort to make them do so, mainly because there never seemed to have been a golden opportunity.

A figure passed in the corridor outside, moving from left to right across Lee's line of vision. In five seconds he registered in his mind that he was looking at a young woman, blonde and hatless, wearing a mustard-coloured suit and carrying a black handbag. Nothing very odd about this: the odd part came a few seconds later when she stopped and glanced back over her shoulder. In that moment Lee recognised her — and she him, apparently. For the briefest instant their eyes met, then they went on up the corridor, moving unsteadily with the swaying of the train.

Lee stirred and looked across at Dale. The big fellow was still busy studying calculations, the light above his head giving a sheen to his bald pate. His bulldog face was in shadow, averted as he bent over the figures.

Lee ventured, 'Er — Mr. Dale — '

'Well, what is it?' Dale did not trouble to look up.

'Does it interest you to know that Miss Elton is on this train?'

'Elton?' Dale's craggy face came into view, masked in thought. 'Elton? Who the hell's — You don't mean *Janice* Elton, that no-good ex-secretary of mine?'

'Either her or her double,' Lee said mildly. 'She just went along the corridor.'

Dale debated this for a moment, then he shrugged fleshy shoulders.

'Well, frankly, I couldn't care less. Nothing to stop her taking the train for Scotland if she wants.' The bushy eyebrows notched suddenly. 'Mmm, it's a bit odd, though. She knew I was taking the train tonight, and she also knows that I'm visiting Highland Amalgamated tomorrow. It was in the appointments book for her to

4

see before I fired her.'

'Yes, sir,' Lee said quietly; then he jumped a little as a train slammed and roared in the opposite direction.

Dale returned to his computations, then at length he put the sheets of paper down on the seat beside him and gave a gesture of exasperation.

'Damned train's shaking so much I can't keep my pen still.' He capped it and thrust it in his breast pocket 'Maybe I'd better give up — Look, Lee, you've got all the details of the Colwin Merger, haven't you?'

'Everything, sir.' Lee touched the brief-case beside him.

'And the estimates for the Pentland Project?'

'Worked out to the last detail, Mr. Dale.'

'Mmm . . . ' Dale gave a heavy smile that did little to iron out the bulldog characteristics of his face. 'You never make a mistake in matters like that, do you, Lee?'

'Never, sir.' Lee smiled faintly and tapped the window frame. 'Touch wood.'

'I could say that I don't know what I'd do without you, Lee — but I won't. Mainly because nobody is really indispensable. Just the same, you're my right hand man. I will admit that much.'

'Thank you, sir.'

'Now look, about the Pentland Project, I think we ought to tell Benson tomorrow that we're — '

Dale stopped. A woman was looking through the one clear space of window that gave on to the corridor — a blonde woman in a mustard coloured suit with a big black handbag under her arm. Dale gazed at her in surprise for a moment, then he surged to his feet and slid the door back.

'Well, Miss Elton?' His voice was coldly courteous. 'Is there something you want?'

She did not answer immediately. She was a good-looking girl in the late twenties, but somehow she had none of the vitality normal to a girl of her age. Her grey eyes seemed cloudily tired, and there was a droop to her delicately made-up mouth and features. She stood appraising Dale's great figure as he stood just within the compartment looking out on her.

'Matter of fact,' she said at length, 'I've been looking up and down the train for you. It wasn't until I caught a glimpse of Mr. Lee a moment ago that I realised you must be here . . . I'd like a few words with you.'

'Oh?'

'In private, if you don't mind.'

'You pick the oddest places.'

'Oh, I don't know. A train compartment is the most private spot in the world.'

'And for that reason you chose the Scots Express because you knew I'd be travelling on it tonight?'

'Since you ask me, yes. I've something very urgent to tell you.'

Dale seemed to come to a decision. 'Look, Miss Elton, when I dismissed you from my organisation our business association ended. You can't have anything further to say to me — and I certainly have nothing to say to you. So, if you'll excuse me . . .'

'This concerns your private life, Mr.

Dale. Something which I must tell you, and which it will be to your advantage to hear.' The girl's grey eyes strayed to Martin Lee as he sat listening. 'I'm quite sure you wouldn't wish it to go . . . any further.'

Silence for a moment, except for the distant scream of the engine whistle and the rhythm of wheels over the rail joints.

'All right,' Dale said finally, shrugging. 'I'll spare you a few moments. Lee, find something to do elsewhere. I'll be finished in five minutes.'

The chief clerk said nothing. Getting to his feet he left the compartment and went out into the corridor. The girl passed inside and took the seat he had been occupying, Dale slammed the door shut and resumed his corner, looking at the girl in the diagonal light of the reading lamp. He was puzzled, very much so, but not for a moment did he show that he was.

'Well, Miss Elton?' he asked presently.

'Mr. Dale, you dismissed me from your organisation because of certain irregularities in my behaviour — '

'I dismissed you because you didn't know how to conduct yourself!' Dale snapped. 'I had no quarrel with your capabilities as a secretary, but I *had* with your misplaced romanticism. Several times — let's face it — you made love to me, and even though I did not reciprocate your behaviour became the talk of the staff. I had to *stop* it, and I did . . . I am a respectable married man with three grown-up children. I have a position that dare not be tarnished by the least hint of scandal. I love my wife, and I have no time for your sort — Clear?'

'You never mince words, do you, Mr. Dale?'

'Never!' He stared at her tired face, his mouth set like a steel trap.

'In fact,' she went on, 'you're something of a paragon among men — or at least you like to think of yourself in that light. You can hire and fire as you please, and nobody dare do a thing about it. Except one person, that is . . . Me.'

'What do you mean by that?'

'I'm going to tell you something, Mr. Dale . . . ' Janice Elton sat back, and relaxed a little, her handbag beside her. 'I admit all you've said is true — that I did try to find some sentimental streaks in your ox-hide makeup, and I think I'd have succeeded too if you hadn't have put your wife and business first. That's as may be, and it's forgotten now. You fired me a fortnight ago, and I haven't got another job yet.'

'That's no concern of mine. I'll give you a business reference anytime, and say nothing of your — amorous qualifications.'

'I haven't taken another job, or even tried for one, because I've been ill. I only started getting around again the day before yesterday.'

'So?'

'I have been told that I have leukaemia, and at the very most I haven't much more than a year to live.'

Dale stared at the floor and cleared his throat roughly. Then he glanced at the girl.

'I'm sorry to hear that, Miss Elton, believe me. No matter what our own personal differences I am genuinely sorry,

10

and that's the truth.'

'I'm sure it is. You know, I got to *thinking* after an edict like that. Well, who wouldn't? I reckoned up and found that I have enough to last me financially as long as I need it — twelve months, that is. But . . . '

'Yes?' Dale prompted, as the girl hesitated.

'I didn't like the way you treated me, Mr. Dale.'

Dale laughed shortly. 'We don't have to go into all that again, do we? I told you why I rid myself of you, and — '

'Yes, but no woman — not my type, anyway — likes to be brushed off as of no account, and dismissed into the bargain. Since I haven't got longer than a year I could easily shorten it and leave you something to remember me by . . . something that I think will knock you from that high perch you're sitting on.'

Dale stared in surprise. 'What are you talking about?'

'It's simple. I tried to make you have me as I am — alive, and as far as I knew at that time good for a long life. Since

11

that didn't work out you can still be made to have me . . . dead.'

Dale was silent, wondering what was coming next. He watched the girl as she opened her handbag deliberately and took from it a small cardboard container. Discarding the container she produced a small bottle of blue glass with a red label affixed. A vague notion of what she intended doing leapt into Dale's mind.

The train lurched as it swung round a bend. The beating of the wheels over the rail joints became a staccato confusion as points were negotiated. Out in the corridor Martin Lee was tipped towards the window. He gazed out into the smother of steam and smoke with the lights of a station streaking through the pall — then he looked at his watch. The five minutes stipulated by his employer had expired, but as yet neither Dale nor Janice Elton had come out of the closed compartment.

Lee began to move. In a matter of fifteen minutes the train would be in Glasgow and he and his boss had one or two details yet to clear up. He reached the compartment, which had always been within his vision anyway, and looked at the closed door. Then he looked at the windows. Blinds were drawn over each one, including the one that had formerly been up.

For a moment Lee listened at the door. As far as he could tell above the creaking and roaring of the train there was no sound of voices. Queer. Finally he knocked lightly and called:

'Mr. Dale, are you there? It's Lee.'

A brief pause, then with a snap of the lock the door slid back and Dale was standing there, a most extraordinary expression on his bulldog face and a blue bottle in his hand.

'What — ' Lee began, but he got no further as Dale bundled him into the compartment and closed the door quickly.

'What's wrong, sir?' Lee demanded, then his gaze moved to Janice Elton. She was in a corner of the compartment, her shoulders wedged into the upholstery and her head lolling forward. It sagged curiously with the motion of the train.

Lee shot a glance at Dale's troubled face. 'What's the matter with her, sir? Is

13

she asleep, or drugged, or — what?'

'She's dead! That's why I drew the blind. I didn't want anybody to see in.'

'Dead!' Lee gave a start. 'You mean she — '

'I mean she committed suicide before I had time to realise what she was up to. See this — ' Dale held out the blue bottle. 'This is what she took — strychnine. She emptied the bottle before I had a chance to stop her. There were brief convulsions and then . . . ' Silence.

'But — but *why?* And in your reserved compartment!' Lee looked up in bewilderment. 'You pulled the communication cord, I suppose?'

'Not yet.' Dale sat down heavily in the corner. 'I did think of it but everything happened so fast. Anyway, what's the use? She's dead. No chance to remedy anything. It only happened a moment or two before you knocked. I haven't had a chance to even think straight.'

Lee reached towards the communication cord, then he hesitated and apparently changed his mind. Moving to the girl he satisfied himself by taking her wrist and

14

feeling at the motionless pulse. There wasn't any doubt about it . . .

'It was deliberate,' Dale said, recovering himself and looking at the bottle in his hand.

'Deliberate?' Lee repeated, and the financier looked at him.

'That's what I said. She told me she'd only a year to live in any case, and to get her own back on me for past injustices — entirely imaginary, I might add — she deliberately killed herself here, intending no doubt to leave me to explain things.'

'Which, of course, you will?' Lee straightened up slowly from beside the girl, his mind aware of certain possibilities.

'Of course I will, you idiot! Pull that cord — we'd better get the guard.'

Lee said slowly, 'Do you think that we ought to be that hasty, Mr. Dale? You're always level-headed in a crisis, and this time there definitely is one. For one thing, you've got that bottle in your hand with the strychnine label on it. Where's the guarantee that Miss Elton took the stuff herself?'

15

'You don't think *I* forced it down her throat, do you? I was compelled to snatch the bottle *away* from her — just as anybody would have done.'

'Yes, I know, but the police might think differently.' Lee sat down slowly beside the financier, his eyes on the dead girl. She was still rocking like an abandoned rag doll under the motion of the train.

'Look,' Dale said, 'this is a deliberate frame-up to get me in a mess — and the quickest way out is to tell the truth.'

'It may be the quickest, but it isn't the safest,' Lee said, with a curious gentleness. 'You say the girl deliberately killed herself to get her own back on you?'

'That's what she said. It's ridiculous, but horribly true. She said something about her having leukaemia and only a year to live — and she also said that since I wouldn't have her alive I could have her dead.'

'Mmm . . . Hell hath no fury like a woman scorned. Be that as it may, and taking into account that she may have been a bit unbalanced mentally by knowing her demise was only a year off, it doesn't alter the fact that you *could* have killed her.'

Dale's face became ugly. 'Now listen, Lee, I never killed anybody in all my life — or even hurt 'em knowingly. I'm willing to take my chance on that score.'

'You are? With a business reputation like yours? Even if the police believe you there's going to be a lot of publicity, and it won't be exactly — favourable. Apart from that strychnine bottle, which by now has got your fingerprints all over it — '

'Damnit, what else do you expect? I told you, I snatched it from her.'

'I'm sure you did, sir, but your fingerprints are all over it just the same. I was saying — apart from that you can be pretty sure that she'll have fixed a lot of other things in advance which will tend to incriminate you once they're unearthed. If she meant to get you — and knowing she was going to commit suicide anyway — she had no need to pull her punches . . . '

The monotonous clicking of the rail joints was not so swift as it had been. The train was commencing to slow down, Dale still looked as though he wondered what had hit him, whereas Lee had a faint smile on his thin features.

'Yes,' Lee said at length, 'she'll have fixed all sorts of things to make matters difficult for you. Let's take a look at her handbag for a start.'

'That's crazy! If the police are to be told we don't want to touch anything — '

'I'm thinking of your interests, Mr. Dale. You've called me your right hand. You need one now if ever you did.'

Lee did not hesitate any further. He lifted the girl's handbag, snapped the catch, and turned the whole issue upside down on the seat. A variety of feminine fripperies fell out. including a small sum of money and, rather significantly, a single ticket to Glasgow. But there was also a sealed envelope, inscribed to 'Whomever It May Concern'. Lee frowned, tore the flap, and pulled out a note. He read it, then without a word handed it to his worried employer.

Dale scowled over it, his jaw setting.

To Whom It May Concern —
In the event of anything happening to

me, please investigate the movements of my former employer, Mr. Morgan Dale, financier, 42 Justin's Court, London, W.1, which person I believe may be directly responsible for any harm that might befall me.

Janice Elton.

'Of all the damned impudence!' Dale snorted, jumping to his feet and throwing the letter on the seat.

'Not so much impudence, sir, as strategy. Evidently she hoped the police would find this note — and you can be sure, as I said earlier, that she'll have left a thorny trail against you.'

'I don't care if she has. The police can think what they like but I intend to tell the truth. Take this bottle, for instance. She couldn't have got poison like this without signing for it. That's one prop kicked from under her precious story to begin with.'

'Look, sir, this is one case where honesty and the facts against you don't jell very easily. Why take a risk like that when everything can be so easily taken care of?'

'How? This is my compartment, reserved in my name, and this girl is inside it — dead.'

Lee got up again and moving to the outer windows he peered round the blind. There were slowly moving, dancing lights in the distance. He turned, obviously thinking swiftly.

'We haven't much time, sir. We're coming to the station . . . Are you prepared to trust me?'

'I've done so for twenty years so I may as well go on doing it. What do you suggest?'

'Throwing this unfortunate young lady out of the carriage whilst there is still time. Since she's dead it won't hurt her.'

'How the devil do you propose to do that? There is solid window on this side of the carriage and the corridor on the other.'

'We're in the last compartment, aren't we? In the corridor there's the door and a drop-window: we wouldn't have to pass any other compartments to get to it. It's a chance, I know, but it's worth it.'

Dale did not say anything. Lee continued:

'In her fingers, which are not yet too rigid, we can put the poison bottle so she'll be clutching it. The handbag and the letter we'll retain. She could hardly jump from a moving train with a handbag clutched to her, but she *might* hold the poison bottle.'

'Mmm — she might. It's ghoulish, Lee.'

'Why is it? It makes you safe, and the girl herself will feel nothing.'

'It *would* make things simpler,' Dale mused.

'Even more so when I swear — should it ever be needed — that you and I were alone in here throughout the journey . . . I'm your right hand man, remember?'

Dale did not hesitate any longer. Indeed there was not the time. In a matter of minutes the train would be pulling into Glasgow. He moved to Lee's side and watched impatiently whilst Lee worked the blue bottle into the girl's stiffening fingers. In the midst of the job he glanced up.

'See if the corridor's quiet,' he instructed. 'If it is, get the door open and leave it on the second catch. We've got to act fast.'

Dale did as he was told — for a change. The corridor was empty. He leapt across the brief stretch to the outside door and dropped the window, reaching his hand down to the outer catch of the door. Steam and cold wind blew into his eyes . . . Then he came back into the compartment to find Lee in the act of hauling the girl's dead weight from the seat.

'Okay,' Lee wheezed. 'Out with her. Grab hold.'

Dale obeyed and grabbed the girl's ankles. Then with the body slumped between them they shuffled quickly across the small intervening stretch of still deserted corridor to the partly unlatched door.

'Right,' Lee panted. 'Leave her to me. I've got her.'

With an effort Lee propped the girl up on her feet, taking her sagging weight against his own shoulder. He reached with one hand to open the door, and then shoved. The door opened slowly against the pressure of the wind and the girl reeled outwards into the night and was gone. The door slammed shut again as Lee pulled it.

He looked at Dale and they went back into their compartment, mopping their sweating faces. At last Dale said:

'I still don't know if we did the right thing.'

'There was no other way, sir — and good luck was with us in that the corridor was empty.'

Lee looked about him and then methodically collected the odds and ends from the seat, the accusing note included, and put them all back in the handbag together with the strychnine bottle's cardboard container. Still with the same calmness he put the handbag in his briefcase and buckled the straps.

'It would be better if I kept the handbag,' he said, as Dale watched him. 'You mustn't have the slightest hint of that girl having been anywhere near you. At a convenient moment I'll destroy everything.'

'Fair enough,' Dale muttered, pulling his hat and coat from the rack. 'Better start getting ready, Lee — we're coming into the station from the look of things.'

Lee said nothing. For a reason best known to himself he was smiling . . .

2

Blackmail

Because at heart he was a straightforward man, the affair of Janice Elton weighed heavily on Morgan Dale's mind. He kept thinking about her, about the ruthless dumping of her corpse on the railway track. It was a memory that kept returning to him, all the time he was busy with business negotiations in Scotland . . . The next day there was only the briefest announcement about her in the newspaper: her body had been found but as yet her identity was unknown.

'But they *will* find out who she is,' Dale insisted the next evening to Lee. 'They're bound to! Laundry marks, or some item like that. They'll discover in time that she was once my personal secretary — and from there the thing will go on.'

'Let it.' Lee shrugged, apparently quite indifferent. 'They can't do a thing to you, sir, not as long as I'm willing to swear that you were with me all the time. Don't *worry* so.'

Dale said nothing. He stared at the end of his cigar absently as he held it in his hand. He and Lee were in the lounge of their hotel, clearing up the final details before their return to London on the morrow.

'Y'know,' Dale said finally, 'the police will be bound to find out that I booked a compartment on the Scots Express. They will assume it more than unusual that my ex-secretary should be on the same train.'

Lee gave his slow smile. 'They can assume all they like, sir, but the law cannot operate on an assumption — only on incontestable facts and witnesses. Otherwise you're protected by the provision of the 'reasonable doubt'. Anyway, it's not certain that she fell from the Scots Express. It's not even certain that she fell from a train at all.'

'Her scratches and bruises where she hit the gravel chippings will be all the police will need in that direction . . . The police are not a gang of halfwits,

Lee; they'll find out from the booking office or somewhere that Janice took the Scots Express. It may be months before they do find out — but they will.'

'If you're determined to worry yourself to a shadow, sir, I'm afraid there isn't much I can do.'

'I can't help *but* worry. I almost feel as though I really murdered her.'

'But you didn't, sir — so you say.'

Dale stared. 'So I *say*! Good God, man, you believe me, don't you?'

'Implicitly, sir. And the police, if they ever catch up, will have to do the same thing — which they will with me to back you up.' Lee reflected over something, then he said quietly, 'We'd better fix up these business matters, hadn't we, sir?'

'Yes, I suppose so . . . ' Dale made a bothered movement. 'Wish I could concentrate better.'

Somehow he succeeded in dissociating his mind from the real problem and gave all his attention to the matter on hand — but the moment he relaxed the old ghost returned. Throughout the night, as he tried to sleep, he kept seeing the body of Janice Elton disappearing through the train doorway into the night. He wished he had the detachment of Martin Lee — but then, when he came to think of it, Lee could afford to be detached. He had been out in the corridor when the girl had killed herself, therefore he had nothing particular to worry about.

Dale felt better when he got back to London and placed something like two hundred and fifty miles between himself and the scene of the tragedy. It gave him a sense of security, however false, and as day succeeded day he managed to so involve himself in business affairs that the fate of Janice Elton touched him but little. He even felt proud that he had not betrayed his secret worry in any way. His wife had not the least suspicion that he was troubled about anything, and his children were all married and away from home so he didn't have to bother to hide his feelings from them. The only person who knew anything was Martin Lee and he seemed as though he couldn't care less and never referred to the matter — unless it was to draw Dale's attention to some item of newspaper news, which he might have missed. Usually, he hadn't; no man was more avid for a newspaper than Morgan Dale.

The disturbing fact was that the police were apparently making progress in their 'body on the line' problem. They had got as far as discovering that the girl, still unidentified, had been thrown from a train after being murdered. Her various abrasions, according to the forensic department, proved this. Also, pathology had shown that strychnine had been administered in a dose of 11.75 grains — and the last thing the police seemed to believe was the possibility of suicide. Nor was there any mention of the poison bottle being found in her clenched fingers . . .

Disquieting facts, which gave Morgan Dale a good deal to think about. The only thing he could cling to was the obvious one: that he had not committed murder or even touched the girl.

Then, a fortnight after the events on the Scots Express, things took a turn — and in a most unpleasant way as far as

Morgan Dale was concerned. He was busy in his private office one morning when Lee entered, thin, smiling, with a curious glitter of satisfaction in his eyes.

'Yes?' Dale asked briefly, without looking up from the work at his desk. 'Something you, want, Lee?'

'As a matter of fact there is.'

The way the words were spoken, and without the usual 'sir', made Dale look up slowly in surprise. He eyed Lee, standing as subservient as ever, at the other side of the desk.

'As a matter of fact I've bought a house,' Lee said. 'I thought you might be interested.'

'Interested?' Dale repeated vaguely. 'Why yes, of course I am. Where is it exactly?'

'It's in a high class part of London. The wife thinks it's beautiful, and so do I. It will save me a great deal of time in getting to the office.'

'Good! Congratulations, Lee. You must have saved pretty hard to enable you to do a thing like that.'

Lee smiled. 'As a matter of fact it's

going to cost around five thousand pounds.'

'Really? That's a lot of money, Lee. What happened? Did you come into a legacy, or something?'

'No; nothing like that. The house isn't paid for yet, but it will have to be by noon tomorrow, or I won't get it. And that would be a big disappointment.'

'Yes, of course it would. But where are you going to get that kind of money? Five thousand pounds doesn't grow on trees. Frankly, what possessed you to embark on such a fantastic scheme when you knew you couldn't afford it?'

'But I can, Mr. Dale — or, to be more exact, *you* can.'

Dale threw down his pen on the rack. The vagueness had left his face and the normal bulldog look had returned. He impaled Lee with cold grey eyes,

'*I* can? What the devil do you mean by that?'

'It has been said, rather truthfully I think, that the labourer is worthy of his hire . . . I'm the labourer.'

'What the hell are you talking about?'

Lee pulled up a chair and sat down indolently, a thing he had never done before in his employer's office.

'I'm talking about Janice Elton, who was thrown from the Scots Express. I'm your right hand man, the only man who can swear you never left my side during the time she died. In a word, I'm your only hope between freedom and a hangman's rope.'

'Stop talking like a melodramatic idiot!'

'Melodrama isn't intended, Mr. Dale — only facts.' Lee grinned irritatingly. 'Those facts have the unfortunate habit of staring one in the face — '

'Now look here, you needn't start trying to intimidate me, Lee. I'm not the sort you can easily frighten. Even if the police get this far — which I doubt — you can't nail me down for anything. The 'reasonable doubt', remember? You said so yourself.'

'I know, but if I am forced to be un-pleasant — which I don't want to be — the police may discover Janice's hand-bag, the note inside it — minus the envelope now, unfortunately — and even the empty bottle of strychnine. You'll have your hands full explaining those away, particularly the bottle with your prints all over it, and hers when she struggled to stop you.'

'When she *what?*'

Dale sat like an image for a moment, somehow unable to credit that the words were coming from his meek and mild head clerk.

'You see,' Lee continued, 'I didn't really put the bottle in Janice's hand. You couldn't really see what I was doing because I told you to go and get the door open — and I tucked her 'bottle hand' out of sight inside her jacket when we carried her . . . I felt that the bottle might be a good lever later on, and I guessed right. And I didn't destroy her handbag either. I still have it intact. Forgive me if I don't say where.'

'So that's your game!' Dale said at last, taking a deep breath. 'Well, I'll admit one thing, I would never have thought you deep enough to try anything so dangerous as blackmail. For that's what it is! You realize that?'

'Of course — but I prefer 'business

arrangement'. It doesn't sound quite so odious.'

'And you know what happens to blackmailers, don't you?'

'Certainly I do. I've examined the situation thoroughly, and I have decided that in this case it's a reasonable risk. If you are silly enough to tell the police about me you'll also have to tell them about Janice — and explain away the evidence, which I'll produce. No doubt I'll suffer, but not half as much as you will. On the other hand, for five thousand pounds you can have peace and . . . ' Lee lighted a cigarette. 'Peace and my unswerving loyalty.'

Dale got up suddenly. He came round the desk in two strides, gripped Lee by the lapels of his jacket and hauled him out of his chair. His cigarette spilled to the carpet.

'Now listen to me,' Dale breathed, pinning him to the wall. 'I'm not being a party to your demands, and what's more I'm going to give you something for your trouble. I'll — '

There was a tap on the door. With an

effort Lee called, 'Come in.'

Perforce Dale had to release his hold, and Lee took good care to place a reasonable distance between himself and his employer. He remained grimly passive as a girl clerk came in, a letter in her hand.

'For you to sign, Mr. Dale. That letter to Phillips.'

'Eh?' Dale looked at her as though he wondered who she was.

'Oh, yes! The letter to Phillips. Thanks.'

The girl gave a vaguely puzzled glance from one to the other and then went out again and closed the door. Lee moved forward, recovered his smouldering cigarette from the carpet, and crushed it in the ashtray. In stony calmness he looked at Dale as he pinched finger and thumb to his eyes.

'The little exercise in primitive emotions being over, Mr. Dale, let me underline what I've said. I want five thousand pounds by tomorrow morning at the latest — and I *don't* want a cheque. Give me that, and you have a guarantor for your movements when Janice Elton died.'

'From the way you talk,' Dale snapped,

'one would think I really *did* murder her.'

'There's only your word for it that you didn't, isn't there? Of course, if you prefer to do battle with the law when it catches up instead of giving me a cent, that's up to you — but I'll make it very hard for you, Mr. Dale, Very hard.'

Dale moved to the desk and sat down heavily. He sat looking at Lee fixedly for a moment before he spoke.

'The thing to do at this moment, Lee, is ask a question — the same question that all victims ask the blackmailer. How do I know you'll keep to your side of the bargain if I pay you five thousand pounds?'

Lee grinned. 'You don't know I will: you'll have to trust me, just as you've done for the last twenty years.'

'Trust you! What an idiot you must think I am! No, Lee, it won't work. Whatever the consequences I'm going to report your behaviour to the police. Now get out, before I kick your miserable hide through that doorway!'

'Obviously, you haven't weighed up every angle,' Lee sighed. 'On what grounds are you going to report me to the police? You haven't a single witness of what I've said, and on my side there are no demands in writing. Threats of extortion, don't they call it? Finally, I'd deny everything, and you'd be left trying to explain away the matter of Janice — her last note to whomsoever it might concern, *and* the poison bottle. Naturally, if you report me to the police I'll give them tremendous assistance without involving myself.'

Dale muttered something under his breath. Aloud he said: 'Quite a schemer, Lee, aren't you?'

'Yes, I rather flatter myself that I am. I play chess a lot, you know — and as the immortal Sherlock once said, that's a sure sign of a scheming mind . . . Your move, Mr. Dale, and your queen is in danger.'

Silence. Dale picked up his ballpoint and studied it absently, and then he put it down again. Lee spread his hands.

'Such a lot of fuss when we can really be quite amicable about it,' he protested. 'You're worth scores of thousands of pounds, Mr. Dale, and five thousand would be a mere button off the shirt to you — yet a fortune to a middle-class clerk like me. Out of it we'd both get peace and quiet . . . Good Lord, it isn't even sensible to haggle over it.'

'You detestable little rat,' Dale whispered.

Lee shrugged. 'All right, so I'm a rat. I don't blame you for letting off steam, but I'm adamant just the same. When you make a mistake like you have you've got to pay for it.'

'I've made no mistake beyond the one of having you for a head clerk. And I did not murder Janice Elton.'

'Don't waste time telling *me*, Mr. Dale. Save it for the police when they get here.'

Through a long interval Dale sat thinking. Finally he slapped his hands palm down on the desk.

'All right, Lee, you've caught me on the hop — but for that five thousand pounds I demand a receipt. I want that poison bottle and Janice's bag with the letter inside it.'

Lee hesitated and then he nodded. 'Very well . . . That still leaves me with a trump card, which I can't possibly give you.'

'Trump card? What are you talking about?'

'I'm talking about myself. I'm your witness, remember? I *could* deny that you were ever with me if it suited my purpose.'

'But I'm paying you five thousand pounds to swear that you *were*! What kind of a scoundrel are you?'

'I'm no scoundrel; I am merely trying to make money out of the man who's ridden roughshod over me for a very long time. All right, you'll get your receipt, but the rest I reserve to myself.'

'So you can bleed me again when the mood seizes you?'

'I'm sorry you have such a poor opinion of my honour, Mr. Dale. Don't worry; you've nothing to fear, and I shall expect the money by tomorrow morning at the latest — in cash, as I said before.'

'It'll be here this afternoon,' Dale snapped. 'When you go for lunch don't forget that you've two things to bring back with you — the handbag and the poison bottle. I was a damned fool to let you take charge of them in the first place.'

'Just one of those things,' Lee smiled. 'On the other hand, if you had had them in your possession and for some reason the police had suddenly swooped, it would have been — well, awkward, wouldn't it?'

'Oh, get out of here!' Dale exclaimed bitterly. 'Get back to your own office and stop there!'

'I'll have to come in now and again in the ordinary course of business, I'm afraid.'

'Make it as seldom as possible!'

Lee went, the smile still on his thin features . . .

3

Carnforth's Wood

It was half past two when Martin Lee reappeared in Dale's office. He found Dale grimly silent, working at his desk, his steel-trap mouth set tightly. For a long time he took no notice of Lee's entrance, but his eyes shifted quickly to the end of the desk as Lee finally laid two objects upon it — quietly, unobtrusively, as though he were laying down a letter to be signed. They comprised a blue poison bottle clearly marked 'Strychnine', and a big black handbag.

'Yours, I think,' Lee said calmly — and waited.

Dale cleared his throat, reached a cigar from the box, and bit the end off impatiently. He raised his eyes at last to find Lee smiling down on him like an archangel.

'Everything's there,' Lee said. 'The

bottle, and the handbag with everything inside.'

Dale did not speak. He picked up the bag, snapped the catch, and tipped the whole issue upside down. The same feminine fripperies as before fell out on the blotter, including the 'To Whom It May Concern' letter and the one-way ticket to Glasgow.

'Correct?' Lee asked politely.

'Shut up!'

Dale put the miscellany back in the bag and then looked at the poison bottle. Finally he picked it up and revolved it slowly in his hand,

'Strychnine — Janice Elton, for the use of,' Lee grinned; then the grin disappeared as he realized the army idiom was not approved of.

'All right,' Dale said at last, unlocking a drawer in his desk. 'There you are — five thousand pounds in cash. Take it and get out of here!'

Lee picked the notes up, variously contrived in fives, tens, and ones. He reflected that they were very dirty notes. With great care he counted them and finally pushed them in his pocket.

'Thank you,' he said calmly. 'Far easier to do it this way than involve ourselves in wrangling, don't you think?'

'I said — get out.' Dale's eyes were dark with menace. 'And do it quickly before I lose control of myself.'

Lee shrugged and moved to the door; then Dale's voice again gave him pause.

'And remember what you're expected to do, Lee. When the time comes for me to call on you to support me — if it ever does — I'm relying on you.'

'But of course.' Lee looked mildly surprised. 'I'll be here — your right hand man.'

He smiled a little, then the office door closed behind him. Dale looked at the panels and bit harder into his cigar. This whole thing was foul and unsavoury — and Martin Lee — with his thin face and sneering smile, the most unsavoury object of all.

'Swine!' Dale muttered, relieving his feelings. 'I'd sooner have a down-to-earth killer than a blackmailer. They crawl from under rocks.'

He stopped muttering to himself and considered the immediate facts. Having obtained the incriminating evidence — at a stiff price — the thing to do was get rid of it, completely and utterly. And this, when Dale came to think of it, was not so easy as it looked. The bag was no problem, nor were the contents, but the poison bottle was a bit of facer. Where he could burn the bag he could not burn the bottle, and if he buried it somewhere, even in the most unlikely place on earth, there are always little boys who'll play at cowboys and dig up the ground, and little dogs who'll root for buried bones, Usually swift in his decisions, Dale was for once at an impasse. He felt himself governed by the fact that he must not make a mistake, and this very necessity clouded his judgment . . . So, for the time being, he put the bottle and bag in his briefcase, locked it, and gave his attention to his business.

That night he took the briefcase home with him and locked it in a drawer in his study. To his wife he was all smiles and genial consideration — in fact rather too much so, for her instincts were gradually aroused as the evening wore on and she caught her husband out in the midst of moody silences. Usually he spent most of the evening reading financial news: this time the stock market seemed the furthest thing from his thoughts.

'Anything the matter, Morgan?' she asked at last, laying aside the novel she was reading.

'Matter?' Dale looked at her absently and then gave a start. 'Matter? Why, no! What gave you that idea?'

'Just a thought. You seemed fathoms deep in something . . . ' Ruth Dale was a quietly smiling woman with greying hair and refined features — a woman whom Dale had always loved and always would. Nothing scandalous must offend her. The fate of Janice Elton must —

'Funny thing about that girl on the railway line, isn't it?' Ruth asked.

'Eh?' Dale blinked twice. 'What girl? What railway line?'

'It's there — in your newspaper. The part turned towards me. The police don't seem to have got much further towards finding out who she is.'

Ruth straightened up and Dale realized she had been reading the opposite side of his newspaper in those few moments. He took a grip on himself and cleared his throat noisily.

'I haven't read the business,' he said, with an effort at sounding casual.

'I don't suppose you have, dear, with so many other things on your mind. I've been following it up — just for curiosity.'

Dale met her eyes. He could see the firelight dancing in them. There was nothing suspicious in their depths; only a kind of vague puzzlement. Dale looked away and turned the newspaper over. With an air of complete disinterest he read the small column about Janice Elton and found it to be merely a résumé of what he knew already . . . nobody knew yet who the girl on the railway line was. But they *would*, finally.

'Interesting, isn't it?' Ruth asked, picking her novel up again. 'As I see it, somebody must have murdered the poor girl and then thrown her from a train. The things people do these days! It's appalling!'

'Yes,' Dale growled, and struggled to his feet. 'Anyway, I've got things to do, Ruth, if you'll excuse me. I'm going into the study for awhile,'

'Very well, dear. There's a good telly programme at half past eight if you want it. A comedy play — '

Dale, at the door, laughed rather shortly. 'For some reason I don't feel like comedy tonight, Ruth. I've other things on my mind.'

With that he left and went across the hall to his study. He entered it, switched on the light, and closed and locked the door. When he had drawn the curtains he took the briefcase from his desk drawer and removed the handbag and bottle.

With the handbag in his fingers he looked about him. There was nowhere here to burn it. Though there was a fire in the lounge — the only fire in the house in fact — there was none anywhere else. Central heating was taking care of the chill of the winter night.

'In any case,' Dale said, half aloud, 'it would be a crazy idea to burn it in the house. It would leave traces, and anyway

46

there'd probably be a smell from the leather, or plastic, or whatever it is.'

This struck him as a new point. He examined the handbag carefully and finally decided it was genuine leather. As he examined it something else occurred to him — Why the devil should he be haunted by this business anyway? He hadn't done anything wrong; Janice Elton had killed herself and nobody else was to blame — and anyway the insidious Martin Lee would stand by him if it came to it. Yes, all truths certainly, but even so Dale felt himself compelled, as though by something other than himself to rid himself of all and everything connected with the girl.

Finally he stood perfectly still, thinking. Somehow, he had *got* to be rid of the bag and bottle, and effectually too. As he stood his mind ranged over a variety of places and finally settled on Carnforth's Wood.

His eyes brightened a little. Yes, why not? Carnforth's Wood was about five miles from his home, a little outcropping off the main road, one of those wooded regions in which all kinds of unknown people dump old mattresses, bedsteads, and ancient chests of drawers . . .

Dale grinned to himself. There certainly would not be anybody around there at this time of year — or this time of night. His mind made up he put the bag and bottle back in his briefcase, strapped and locked it up, and then left the study. He looked in on his wife in the lounge,

'Going to see Bob Allsop, dear,' he announced briefly. 'I've something I want to get straight with him before morning.'

Ruth nodded, engrossed in her novel. Glad that she didn't ask awkward questions Dale closed the lounge door again, scrambled into his hat and coat, and within ten minutes was driving down the main road from his home through a cold, blustering wind.

'All this because of Janice Elton,' he muttered, staring ahead into the brilliant tunnel produced by the headlights. 'What the devil did the girl want to make such a fool of herself for? Panic reaction — that's what it must have been.'

He ceased muttering to himself and

concentrated on his driving. Once he was through the small town where his home was situated he came to the main country road that led, by devious routes, to the major road to London. But long before he reached it he turned off to the left and bounced and bumped for nearly three miles along a badly-made road until he came at last to Carnforth's Wood standing on a corner. He switched off the headlights and sat gazing at the scene — what he could see of it in the night.

The wood itself was separated from the road by an entirely inadequate fence of sagging wire. The trees, some of them still retaining a few charred leaves, were swaying sturdily in the strong wind, and beyond the trees in the immediate foreground was the dim reflection of a pond — a paradise for urchins with jam jars in the summer months.

His survey over, Dale took the handbag and bottle from his briefcase and scrambled out of the car. The thin wind smote him and he turned up his coat collar hastily. He looked about him.

Nothing. Not the remotest sign of life

— unless the two far distant yellow spots which denoted a farmer's cottage could be called life. Nothing that mattered anyhow. He was free to act — and he started by going to the boot of his car and taking out a heavy adjustable spanner and the jack. Then he set to work. He laid a piece of sacking on the hard earth road, a sack used to protect his clothes when engaged on minor repairs — laid the jack upon it, and then the bottle. With the spanner he smashed the bottle into small pieces, and then into crumbling, glittering dust, using the jack as a hard background for the impacts of the spanner, In the end he had nothing left of the bottle save a heap of powder the colour of an amethyst.

'That settles *you!*' he murmured, and the only response was from the dry, dead leaves of the trees as they crackled under the force of the cruel wind.

Dale paused for a moment and looked about him, reassuring himself that all was well. It was. Satisfied, he gathered up the sacking and debris of the bottle, dodged under the absurd slack wire of the fence, and tramped deep into the wood until he came to the pond. Over its ruffled waters he shook the sack vigorously, scattering the blue powder that had been the poison bottle. The label went too — a mangled, pulped mass of ripped paper, which was valueless now as a clue, in any case. This done, he gave the sacking a final shake and retreated once more to the roadway, taking care to scuff out his footprints in the soil as he went. Because of the darkness he couldn't be sure if he did it properly, but he reckoned that rain and wind would complete the job in any case before long.

And now the bag. No use doing anything with that here, the flame of a fire would show for miles in the darkness. It would be more sensible to go back to the office and burn the bag there. There was a grate in his private office and there wouldn't be anybody in the building. By morning, any tell-tale odour there might be would have dispersed anyway.

He put the sacking, jack, and spanner back in the boot, then got into the car once more with the handbag beside him.

He reversed awkwardly down the rutted road until he came to a convenient gap where he could turn, then he put on speed to get back to the properly surfaced road once more.

After that it was easy. In twenty minutes he was in town, drawing up outside his office. He entered it, the handbag in his hand, and strode with easy familiarity through the dark, empty reaches of the general office to his private sanctum. Switching on the light he went over to the fireplace and, screwing up some paper from the w.p.b. nearby, he put the bag on top of it. He reflected for a moment over the money in the bag — a small amount but money just the same. His commercial mind revolted at the idea of burning it, but on the other hand perhaps it was safer.

'Everything!' he insisted to himself. '*Everything* must go!'

Decision reached, he acted. He struck a match, applied it to the paper, and watched the yellow flame lick and ripple round the bag. As he watched, a thought struck him. Where was the cardboard container in which the poison bottle had originally been? Oh well, perhaps it didn't matter very much — he'd destroyed the bottle, and that was the main thing.

The fire in the grate gained a hold rapidly, and he coaxed the burning process with the poker. Finally the whole bag fell to pieces in brown chunks of ash, leaving behind a few fire-defiled pieces of silver and copper, and the skeleton remains of a clasp.

Dale disposed of these last traces effectually when they had cooled sufficiently. He thrust them into cracks of the wall in the old-fashioned coke cellar, where the central heating unit was located. The chances of finding the burned remains down here were practically negligible . . . Then, feeling considerably easier in his mind, he returned to the office to clear away the tell-tale ashes from the grate. He collected them all in a bucket and then placed them in the ash can in the yard, smashing the bigger pieces of burned leather into fine dust with the blade of the shovel.

When he was done he was satisfied that he had done everything a man could do to destroy the evidence, which brought again the question — why?

'I'm beginning to think I really *did* murder Janice from the amount of trouble I'm taking,' he mused to himself, as he prepared to depart. 'Which only goes to show what a frame of mind can do to you!'

He took up his briefcase, lighted a cigarette, and then gave a grim smile. Janice had said that she would leave something to remember her by, and she certainly had. She had left other things than she had intended — nagging doubts, fear, and an immense uncertainty, and a thin, smiling man who contemplated blackmail with the air of an expert.

Dale wondered as he left the building if Martin Lee would be content with what he had got, or would he again reach out greedily — and yet again — bleeding Dale of everything he possessed.

★　★　★

A week passed, a week of ominous quiet so far as developments were concerned.

Dale continued with his work, gaining fresh hope from the lack of startling surprises — and Lee behaved as though nothing had ever happened to cause a hiatus in his career as chief clerk. Yet, somehow, the quietness was unnerving. It produced a queer feeling of anticipation, a not very pleasant anticipation either.

For one thing, Scotland Yard knew now the identity of the body on the line. The newspapers had said as much. For another, they knew that Janice Elton had taken the Scots Express to Glasgow on the night of the tragedy, and that she had presumably been thrown from that train by whoever had killed her. In fact, as Dale and Lee so rightly judged, the police were creeping ever nearer — and about a fortnight after Janice's death they caught up. They did it disarmingly, even pleasantly, in the shape of Chief-Inspector Royden of the Yard, an impassive man with a slightly bald head and toothbrush moustache.

He arrived in Morgan Dale's private office without saying who he was. To the staff he was a businessman on an urgent

55

mission, to Dale he made his identity clear with a warrant card. Then he sat down, the friendliest of smiles on his features, and studied Dale with grey eyes as keen as a rapier.

'This,' Dale said, recovering himself and pushing over the silvered cigarette box, 'is something of a shock, Inspector, I must admit that.'

'A shock?' Royden lighted his cigarette at the lighter that Dale held for him. 'Thanks . . . why should it be — '

'I am not in the habit of expecting the law in my office, Inspector — and anyway it's bad for business.'

'Nobody knows that I'm a police officer, Mr. Dale, except you. We look after the proprieties, you know. And I'm only here on a routine enquiry, otherwise I'd have brought my sergeant along with me.'

'Oh! I see . . . ' Dale sat back in his chair and looked at the Inspector's smooth jowls. 'Er — what exactly do you wish to know? I can't think of anything so amiss with my business that it demands a visit from Scotland Yard.'

'Rest assured, Mr. Dale, that I am not in the least concerned with your business. In fact I don't belong to that department. I'm from Criminal Investigation.'

'So I gathered from your warrant card.' Dale raised his eyebrows. 'Well, what can, I do for you?'

'On the best of information, sir, I believe you once employed a young woman by the name of Janice Elton?'

Dale pondered deliberately. 'Janice Elton? Let me think now . . . Janice Elton . . . '

The Chief-Inspector stabbed smoke with his cigarette. 'It ought not to demand a great effort of memory, Mr. Dale. From my enquiry I find that until recently she was your private and personal secretary.'

'Yes — she was.' Dale saw that hedging was no use. 'I fired her about a month ago. Why? What's she done?'

'She hasn't done anything. Somebody's done something to her — murdered her. My job is to try and find out why, and who it was that killed her.' Royden looked at his cigarette end reflectively. 'Don't you read the papers, Mr. Dale?'

'Not a great deal. I don't pay much attention to news in the ordinary way. I'm more concerned with the stock market information.'

'I see . . . ' The grey eyes stared for a moment. 'In that case I'd better bring you up to date. Janice Elton was murdered on the Scots Express on January 10th. Strychnine was administered, and after that she was thrown from the train.'

'Ghastly,' Dale muttered, quite convincingly. 'Ghastly! It comes as a distinct shock to me since I knew her so well.'

'We managed to trace her identity, and from that we found out that she was formerly your secretary, and that she booked a single ticket to Glasgow on January 10th. From that it would appear that she had no intention of returning from Scotland once she got there. I believe you went to Scotland at the same time — even on the same train?'

'Well, yes . . . ' Dale gazed for a moment. 'Can I ask how you know that?'

'Certainly. Actually we traced the information in Scotland when we came to make inquiries about the passengers on the Scots Express. But apart from that the fact was mentioned in the newspapers — those papers in which you unfortunately don't read the daily news.'

'Oh . . . ' Dale took his cigarette out of his mouth and tapped ash into the brass tray. Then he said hesitantly, 'You're not attaching anything significant to the fact that I went to Scotland at the same time as Janice Elton, are you?'

Royden spread his hands and smiled. 'I am prepared to admit that it was a coincidence . . . for the moment. There was somebody with you, I believe? A business associate perhaps?'

'That would be Mr. Lee, my chief clerk. You'd like to have a few words with him perhaps?'

'No, no . . . ' Royden raised his hand. 'It doesn't signify. I only want to ask a few questions about Janice Elton, then I'll be on my way . . . Tell me, had she any enemies that you know of?'

'None as far as I know. I can't pass any opinion on her private life since I didn't know anything about it.'

'She hadn't a fiancé or boy friend who

might have had reason for wanting to kill her?'

Dale shook his head and kept silent. The Chief-Inspector drew at his cigarette for a moment and then asked:

'What kind of girl *was* Janice?'

'Oh — quite satisfactory, and a good secretary.'

'And yet you dismissed her? We have that information from the Labour Exchange when she handed in her card and became available for secretarial work . . . Why did you fire her, Mr. Dale?'

Dale hesitated. 'You wish me to be absolutely frank?'

'It would be wisest.'

'All right then. She — ' Dale spoke with effort. 'She made love to me on various occasions, so much so that the staff began talking about it. I couldn't tolerate that sort of thing.'

'Why not? There are not many men who object to the amorous advances of a pretty young woman.'

'I don't happen to be that kind of man,' Dale retorted. 'I am a respectable man with a high position to maintain. And I love my wife sincerely. On those grounds I fired Janice before we perhaps got too deeply involved.'

'With you not reciprocating her advances how could you get involved?' Royden asked.

Dale shrugged. 'I'm only human, with all of the failings of the male sex. I didn't trust myself, you understand — so I got rid of temptation before it became too much for me.'

'Mmmm . . . ' Royden crushed out his cigarette in the ashtray and reflected for a moment or two. Then he said, 'Janice Elton was a doomed woman, you know — quite apart from her being murdered.'

'Doomed?' Dale repeated.

'Yes. According to the surgeon who conducted the p.m. on her body she had been suffering from advanced leukaemia, which would have brought about her death anyway in a few months. Her murderer couldn't possibly have known this, of course, otherwise he might have been content to let Nature take its course.'

Dale grasped at a slender thread, 'Are you so sure it was *murder*?' he questioned. 'Hasn't the possibility of suicide ever occurred to you?'

'Of course. Every possibility has occurred to us — insofar as human beings can reason, that is. Suicide doesn't fit because she couldn't have thrown herself out of a train after taking strychnine — and it was *afterwards* because her bruises and abrasions prove the fact. No, Mr. Dale, she was murdered all right.'

Dale was silent, waiting for the next. He sat gazing at the desk, but even so he could feel those rapier eyes passing over him, eyes that were trying to read something, eyes that were trying to probe . . . Then he relaxed slightly. After all — he hadn't done anything really, except destroy a poison bottle and a handbag. Why should he worry . . . ?

'Well,' Royden said, into the silence, 'I don't think I need to take up any more of your time at present, Mr. Dale. If I need more information I'll call upon you again.'

'As you wish,' Dale assented, thankful that the ordeal was over. 'If I can help in any way I'll be glad to.' Royden got to his feet, smiled genially, and shook hands.

Then he left the office. Dale sat for a moment and expelled a vast sigh of relief. He felt that he had got over the first hurdle and that from here on he could handle anything that came his way. Perhaps he could even do without Lee's support —

There was a tap on the door.

'Come in,' Dale said, almost cheerfully — then his expression changed as Martin Lee entered silently, that curiously twisted smile on his thin features.

'Well?' Dale demanded. 'What do you want?'

Lee closed the door and then came forward to the desk. He pondered for a second or two and then asked a question:

'That chap who's just gone. He was from the Yard, wasn't he?'

Dale said deliberately: 'He was a business representative.'

'That's queer . . . ' Lee took a cigarette from the box and lighted it. 'I've never seen business representatives using squad cars before. Perhaps a new gimmick they've thought up.'

'What the devil are you talking about?'

'I'm talking about the man who came to see you. I saw him draw up outside the building: I've a good view from my office, remember, even if nobody else on the staff has. It's not a bit of use you pretending, Dale ... He came from Scotland Yard, didn't he?'

Dale gave a sour smile. 'Don't miss much, Lee, do you? All right, he came from the police about Janice. All he did was ask a few questions about her, such natural ones I didn't even need to defend myself or call upon you.'

'Not yet, that is.' Lee watched smoke drifting to the office ceiling.

'All right, not *yet*,' Dale conceded. 'If things get tough I'll send for you — Now get out, will you? You're a disturbance to my peace of mind.'

Lee chuckled. 'That's a good one! I shouldn't think murderers can *ever* have peace of mind. Unless of course you happen to be the exception.'

Dale's eyes glinted. 'Look, Lee, I've already told you — '

'All right, I know — I know. You didn't even touch Janice Elton and she scoffed the strychnine all by her little self, while you looked on. It's a damned likely story, isn't it?' Lee's face became ugly for a moment as he headed towards the door. 'See you again, Dale, when it becomes necessary to save you from our friend of the law.'

The door closed and Dale sat staring at it in cold hatred.

4

Unexpected Death

It was shortly after lunchtime when Chief-Inspector Royden returned to his rather dingy office overlooking the Thames Embankment. He put his hat and coat on the peg and then looked across at his right-hand man, Detective-Sergeant Mason, busy with a typewriter at his own desk.

'Any luck, sir?' Mason asked, as his superior wandered over to his own desk and lighted a cigarette.

'Sort of a mixed bag . . . ' Royden stared out pensively into the London murk. 'I had a few words with Morgan Dale, but from my first impression I'd say he's as innocent as a baby — and yet *somehow* connected with the death of Janice. It's a bit of a problem.'

Mason wandered over from his own corner. 'What kind of a man *is* Dale, anyway? A typical tycoon?'

'Anything but. Certainly a business-man, but he also has something of the stamp of a family man about him. He's tough and yet he's decent — and certainly he's damned evasive.'

'And yet you think he's innocent?'

'Yes.' Boyden gave a direct look of his grey eyes. 'Yes, I do somehow.' He shrugged. 'Of course, that's only an instinctive feeling and not a bit of good in law, I know, but sometimes it pays off to work on a hunch.'

'Yes — sometimes,' Mason agreed, keeping his feet on the earth.

'I tried him out,' Royden added. 'He told me that Janice had made love to him on several occasions, and that was why he fired her. I suggested that there aren't many men who object to a nice girl making love to them — Well, he rounded on me like a tornado and told me that he wasn't that kind of man, that he loved his wife sincerely, and all the rest of it. I made my remark deliberately to see what he'd do . . . And I found out.'

'Just the same,' Mason said, 'that still doesn't make him innocent. In fact rather the contrary. I should think he'd have rather good reasons for wanting Janice Elton out of the way.'

'Even so, I can't see him as the murdering type. I'll admit he might kill somebody in a sudden fit of passion or impulse — in fact most of us might do that, but from the facts we've got this doesn't seem to be a crime of impulse. It isn't an impulsive crime when you ram strychnine down a girl's throat and then deliberately drop her from a train. It's much too calculated.'

'Is there anybody else involved?' Mason asked. 'Had she any enemies who — '

'I tried that line, and drew a blank. The facts are that she went to Glasgow at the same time as Morgan Dale, that she was once his amorous secretary and fired for that reason, that she had — as you know from reports — a disease which would have killed her anyway in a few months. On the train there was also a Mr. Lee, Dale's chief clerk. That's all we've got at the moment. Somewhere we've got to fit in the strychnine, and the girl's transference from the train to the railway line.

Somebody threw her there — but to find a witness to the act is next to impossible. Pity trains don't keep a passenger list like ships and airplanes.'

'What's next then?' Mason asked.

Royden considered. 'Frankly, I'm not at all sure . . . We could investigate the girl's background to the full — and we probably will before we're finished — but on the other hand we might do better if we had a few words with the only other party in the case. I mean this chap Lee, Dale's chief clerk. He might have a different slant on Janice that will bear hearing. Yes, I'll do that — '

Royden reached to the telephone and in a few minutes was speaking directly to Morgan Dale. Dale, in his private office, listened with taut nerves whilst the Inspector spoke.

'Hello, Mr. Dale. Royden here . . . Look, I'd like a few further words with you regarding this business of Janice Elton . . . '

'With pleasure,' Dale responded, trying to sound affable. 'But what more can I tell you? We covered everything this morning, didn't we?'

'Not entirely. Oh, we did as far as you are concerned, but I think a few words with Mr. Lee might help things. He might know some aspects of Janice Elton which you don't.'

'Er — yes, he might,' Dale agreed doubtfully. 'After all, he's only my chief clerk and he didn't see Janice — '

'Just the same I'll talk to him. In fact I'll talk to you both at the same time. I know you're a busy man — and so presumably is Lee — so which is it to be? Will you come to my office or shall I come to you?'

There was only a fractional hesitation on Dale's part, then he said: 'You'd better come here. I've one or two things which demand my personal attention at the moment — '

'I understand. What would be a convenient time?'

'Say in about an hour. I'll have Lee here for you: he's out at the moment. How's that?'

'I'll be there.'

The line clicked. Dale put the telephone down slowly and sat thinking, his lips tight. The brief relief which had come upon him in the morning when the Chief-Inspector had departed had now vanished. The old worry was back again. He had the same ordeal to go through once again . . . With an effort he forced himself back to realities and snapped the button on his intercom.

'Lee? Come in here a moment.' Then he switched off and waited.

After a moment or two Lee came in. As usual he was smiling with inner confidence. As usual, he took a cigarette from the box on the desk and lighted it. Then, after immense deliberation, he raised his eyebrows enquiringly.

'Well?' he questioned, disregarding the icy look in Dale's eyes.

Dale said: 'Scotland Yard will be back here in an hour and I'll need your full support. They're going to question both of us this time.'

For some reason Lee looked at his watch. 'Half past two,' he murmured. 'Yes, there's just time.'

'Time for what?'

'Time for you to go to the bank. I've held off bothering you until the crucial moment — and now it's here. If I'm to stand by you — my trump card remember — it'll cost you another two thousand pounds, in cash.' Lee flicked ash on the carpet. 'So you'd better get busy, hadn't you?'

Dale smiled — a grim, unyielding smile. 'So I wasn't wrong, was I? Your intention is to bleed me white if you can. Well, Lee, it won't work. You're not getting another cent.'

'Then I won't stand by you. In fact I'll turn things the other way and make you sit up.'

'As you wish.' Dale's craggy face might have been carved out of teak for all the expression he showed. 'It'll be your word against mine and I think Inspector Royden will know which man to believe. I'll stake everything on the one fact that I haven't done anything wrong, and therefore I cannot suffer. On the more material side, I've destroyed every trace of evidence. That's your answer, Lee, and nothing on earth will make me change it.'

Lee took several moments thinking things out, then he finally gave a little shrug and crushed his cigarette in the ashtray.

'Very well,' he said. 'You leave me no alternative. I have things to do . . . ' He moved towards the office door.

'Where are you going?' Dale snapped.

'Out. I've a call to make.'

The door closed sharply and Dale blinked a little. What the call was which Lee had referred to he had no idea. He could only hope that the chief clerk would be back in time for Royden to speak to him. If not, it was up to Royden to find him . . .

His mind cloudy with unpleasant speculations, Dale resumed his normal work and after a time the minutes slipped by unnoticed. It was only when an hour had passed and there was no sign of Lee returning that Dale went impatiently in search of him — without result. Lee was nowhere in the building, and most certainly not in his office, nor had he left any indication of where he intended to go.

'Damned fool,' Dale muttered, returning at length to his own office. 'Now I'll have to explain things to Royden when he arrives . . . ' He glanced at his watch. 'Time he had shown up anyway.'

But another hour passed before Royden finally appeared, and on this occasion he was not alone. Detective-Sergeant Mason was beside him. Dale eyed them as they were shown into his office.

'At least your plain clothes don't give anything away, gentlemen,' he said, motioning to chairs. 'All the same my staff will begin to think. Next time you want me I'd better come to you.'

'Yes,' Royden agreed pleasantly. 'Maybe that would be as well — Oh, this is Detective-Sergeant Mason, my right hand man.'

Dale nodded briefly in acknowledgment and then said: 'I'm afraid your visit is valueless, Inspector, as far as seeing Mr. Lee is concerned. He went out earlier this afternoon, and although I told him you were coming within an hour after your call, he hasn't yet returned.'

'No,' Royden said. 'And I don't think he *will* return, either.'

Dale looked up in surprise. 'No? Why?'

'Because Lee's dead. He was in a traffic

74

accident this afternoon and has since died. That's why I'm late.'

'He's — he's *dead?* But how do you come to be — '

'It's quite simple really. I was on the point of coming here within the hour, as I promised, when there came a call from the General Hospital, to which Lee had been taken. It seemed that in a brief recovery from unconsciousness Lee was asking for me. He had been on his way to see me when the accident happened. Why he wanted me I never discovered since he was dead when I got there.'

'Dead,' Dale whispered, as though he still could not believe it. 'I did mention your name to him, of course, when I told him you would be coming here, but why he should want to see you beforehand I can't imagine.'

Royden said: 'Since Lee is involved posthumously in the matter of Janice Elton I am handling the matter of his death, instead of the ordinary police. I'll see Lee's relatives are notified, and that the driver of the car that killed him is apprehended. However, that's beside the point. As things are I've taken charge of Lee's personal effects.'

'Yes — yes, I see,' Dale said, trying to make up his mind whether Lee's death was an advantage or not.

'Among his effects,' Royden went on, unstrapping the briefcase he was carrying, 'was *this*. I wonder if you can explain it in any way?'

Dale watched in fascination as Royden brought a small cellophane envelope into view. Inside it were two objects — a small cardboard container and a blue poison bottle. It was plain that each belonged to the other although they were separate in the envelope. The bottle had no label.

'Up to now,' Royden said, 'this bottle hasn't been closely examined, but I was struck by the fact that it was in Lee's pocket — inside this container as a matter of fact. From the brief examination I've given it, the bottle contained strychnine.'

Dale stared fixedly, piecing together in his mind what the explanation must be. Obviously Martin Lee had switched bottles — taken the label off this one and transferred it to the duplicate bottle, which he — Dale — had been at such pains to destroy. The one in the envelope hardly needed a label to prove that it had contained strychnine. Analysis would prove that quickly enough.

'It is singular,' Royden said, 'that Janice Elton died of strychnine poisoning and that the bottle, which has never been located so far, should turn up in Lee's pocket. I admit it may be coincidence and perhaps has nothing to do with the business, but the facts are quite remarkable. Lee travelled on the same train as yourself and Janice; he was employed by you, as she was, and she was killed by strychnine — which this bottle has contained. However, maybe we'll know a bit more when we've had 'Dabs' take a look at the bottle.'

'Dabs?' Dale repeated, and Royden laughed slightly.

'Forgive me — the Fingerprint Department, to give its full and august title.' He laid the envelope on the desk, considered the contents, and then pulled forth his cigarette case and proffered it. 'My turn,' he said, smiling.

'Thanks,' Dale said absently, then he apologised suddenly as he fumbled the cigarette and knocked the case to the desk. He handed it back, then pulled one of the weeds from under the stiff metal fastener.

'There's no need to be nervous, Mr. Dale,' Royden said, snapping his lighter into flame. 'Disturbing though the police may be there's no intention of frightening anybody to death — even less so when the party concerned is innocent.'

Dale relaxed a little. After all he *was* innocent. Why then did things keep piling up on top of him in this way?

'Then you've no idea how Lee came to have this bottle on him?' Royden asked, after a moment.

'No idea at all.' Dale shook his bald head. 'He never even mentioned a poison bottle in his conversations with me.'

'Conversations? What kind of conversations?'

'Oh, nothing particular. Just this and that . . . '

'I see . . . ' The Chief-Inspector was looking good-humoured again. 'Y'know, if Lee was coming to see me I'll wager it was because of this bottle, which for some reason he wanted to keep secret from you. Otherwise it would have been time enough when I turned up to keep my appointment.'

Dale said nothing. He knew exactly what Lee had intended — to blacken the case beforehand, because he had not got the two thousand pounds he had demanded.

'On the other hand,' Royden mused, 'he might have wished to make a statement of some kind, hence his anxiety to see me . . . Well, we'll never know now what he intended.' He sighed, put the cellophane envelope and its contents back in the briefcase and then strapped it up again.

'There's nothing more you wish to ask?' Dale enquired.

'Not at the moment. I only wanted to know about this bottle, and to tell you personally about Lee. I don't think there's anything more for the moment, Mr. Dale, so I'll be on my way.'

Dale nodded, shook hands with both

men, and watched them go. The one thought buzzing through his mind was that Lee was *dead*, therefore there would be no more blackmailing demands; but on the other hand there wouldn't be any support, either, to prove that Janice Elton had not been murdered. But then, Lee had said he wouldn't lend his support unless paid for it . . .

'Oh, hell!' Dale muttered, mentally going round in circles. 'Let it sort *itself* out. Why should *I* worry?'

Why indeed? He just could not help but do so; he was in the grip of a tremendous uncertainty as to what the law would do next. In its blind, juggernaut progress, unswayed by sentiments, it might very easily find a way of showing that Dale *had* murdered Janice Elton. Then the fat would be in the fire with a vengeance.

Meanwhile, Royden and Mason were returning to the Yard in the police car, the sergeant at the wheel. As he drove through the imprisoning traffic he made a comment.

'You didn't get much change out of that, did you, sir?'

'No, I'm afraid not.' Royden didn't appear disturbed. 'I thought Dale might produce a definite reaction on seeing this bottle from Lee's pocket, but he didn't. I took you along so I can have an independent assessment of him . . . What do you think?'

'Oh, he seems all right on the face of things — but then, it doesn't pay in our job to judge by appearances. The only thing we can go on is that we haven't any proof against him — and if that sounds Irish I apologize.'

'There *is* the possibility that Lee wanted to confess to the murder of Janice Elton and was on his way to do so when he was knocked down,' Royden mused. 'But then again that raises the question — why *should* he confess? A murderer doesn't do that without a very good reason, and I can't see one as far as Lee was concerned.'

'What's the next move then?' Mason asked, driving onwards through the traffic.

'Have Dabs take a look at this bottle and container. That might start something anyway. We've got a good set of prints from Dale which will do for a start.'

'Taken, I assume, when you handed him your cigarette case?'

'Naturally.' Royden gave a sigh, 'Unfortunately it's one of the anomalies of law that you can't fingerprint anybody openly until there's a conviction. Makes you wonder what they'll think of next to hinder hard-working policemen.' He frowned slightly. 'Queer there's no label on the bottle, though . . . '

'What about Janice's prints? Have we got any of hers?'

'Sort of — taken from her dead hand. They're not as clear as the living flesh would have made them, of course, but if we need to we can always get another set from where she lived. Everything's sealed off so there won't be anything disturbed.'

By this time the Yard had been reached, and Royden didn't waste any time in transferring bottle and container within their cellophane envelope to the finger-print department. This done, he considered for a moment or two and Mason stood waiting expectantly.

'Be a little time before we get a result on that,' Royden said, 'and if there's one thing I can't stand it's wasting time . . . Let's consider for a moment: of the two people in the field likely to have given Janice poison we have Lee and Morgan Dale — in that order. Let's see now . . . '

Royden looked at the notes he had made, then sucked his teeth in annoyance.

'Damn! The bottle's got no label, which probably would have had the chemist's name and address on it. It doesn't always apply, of course, if the poison is bought ready made up — All we've got to go on is the Hexley Chemical Company of Wolverhampton, who presumably are the manufacturing chemists selling their products to the retail chemists. Mmm, that means we'll have to inquire of all the chemists around the homes of Lee and Dale if either of them bought strychnine lately. It'll have to be in the poison book records.'

'True,' Mason acknowledged, 'but what happens if one of them has signed a false name?'

'In that case we'll see if the chemist concerned can remember a person looking like Lee or Dale.' Royden scratched among his papers and then said, 'Here's Lee's address. Hop to the job and see what you can find from the chemists within his area. I'll do the same for Dale in a while. I want to see all the details about Lee's death are taken care of first.'

'Okay . . . ' Mason headed for the door, then paused as he reached it. 'Any time limit for when I'll have to report back?'

'Make it six-thirty, here. You'll not get much satisfaction from the shops after that time.'

Mason nodded and hurried out. The Chief-Inspector was not very long after him, his mind satisfied that the details of Lee's fatal accident were duly being taken care of, and his family notified. Here, this particular phase of the business ended, Royden could give himself up completely to the task of solving the puzzle of Janice Elton's death.

And he had set himself a difficult task, as he had well realized from the start. For all that remained of the afternoon, and part of the evening, he made enquiries from every chemist he could find — in main streets, side streets, little cul-de-sacs and unlikely places, covering everywhere within an area of two miles of Morgan Dale's home, and not a single success did he have. He came back to the Yard looking completely disgusted, to find that Mason had just arrived back.

'Any luck?' Royden put his hat and coat on the peg.

'Not a sausage. Always granting of course that Lee signed in his own name. Plenty of entries for strychnine in the poison books, but none with Lee's name or address.'

'And nobody remembers a man like him?'

'Afraid not.'

'Mmm . . . ' Royden sat at his desk and sighed. 'Well, you haven't done any worse than I have, if that's any consolation to you. No luck for me, either, I've gone down so many roads and in so many shops I'm nearly dizzy. Send out for sandwiches and tea, will you? We may be here quite a while yet.'

'Right, sir.'

As Mason headed out of the office Royden looked at his desk. There upon the blotter was the familiar cellophane bag with its enclosures of bottle and cardboard container. They were on top of a card report. Royden read it thoughtfully:

Report on sample submitted.
(a) poison bottle. There are numerous prints on this, the most obvious being those of Janice Elton (specimen prints submitted by you), and also those of Morgan Dale (prints submitted by you from your cigarette case). There is also a set of further prints which are not identified since there are no comparison prints. (Possibly chemists' prints?)
In regard to the (b) container these contain a great variety of prints, but the only ones we can classify for comparison purposes are those of Janice Elton.

'Very interesting,' Royden murmured to himself. 'Very interesting.'

He got up, put the cellophane bag and contents in a locker, then turned as Mason came back with a tray bearing tea and sandwiches. As the two men disposed of the refreshment Royden outlined what had so far come to light from Dabs.

'From that, then,' the Sergeant said thoughtfully, 'it would appear that Morgan Dale's got a lot to explain. If he's never seen the bottle how on earth did his prints get on it?'

'Obviously, he's lying.' Royden chewed a ham sandwich as he pondered. 'His prints don't seem to be on the cardboard container, however, and that may be important. *Why* important I can't tell you until I've thought it out.'

'Our next job, then, is to have words with Dale again, isn't it, and find out what he's keeping to himself?'

'That can wait for the moment. He'll be there when we want him. The better idea would be to get some specimen prints of Martin Lee and see if they match up anywhere in this little set-up.'

'Whatever you say, sir.'

Royden consumed another sandwich

before he spoke again, and then it was with thoughtful deliberation:

'Know something, Mason? This business of Janice Elton, and her tie-up between Lee and Dale, goes a lot deeper than we first imagined. Up to now we've only dabbled on the fringe of the thing. The real fun and games have yet to come. Tomorrow we're hunting again for the purchaser of strychnine.'

Mason stared. 'But where do we *look*? We've done all that already — unless you intend widening the area?'

'Not at all. Doesn't it occur to you that Janice might have bought the stuff *herself*? It could be, you know — but somebody else administered it.'

5

Further Revelations

The following morning Chief-Inspector Royden, inevitably accompanied by Mason, set two lines of action in motion. First he visited Lee's home, expressed his condolences to a rather sour-faced Mrs. Lee, and deliberately refrained from asking any pertinent questions. That could come later — if necessary. At the moment his main desire was to secure specimen fingerprints, and this he finally managed by taking away Lee's hairbrush. He explained this as a necessity — some hair combings were needed to corroborate a point in the evidence concerning Lee's accident — and of course Mrs. Lee did not try and raise any objection. Either she knew better than to question the authority of a police Inspector, or else she couldn't care less what happened to her late husband's belongings. Somehow, Royden had the impression that the latter was the case.

This done, and with the hairbrush in one of the ubiquitous cellophane bags, Royden went on with the next part of his investigation — the endeavour to trace the purchaser of the strychnine which had killed Janice.

'Don't you think, sir,' Mason ventured, as he drove the car towards the area where the girl's flat lay, 'that it would be a good idea to search Janice's flat from top to bottom?'

'Why?' Ryden asked mildly, cuffing his hat up on his forehead.

'Only that you haven't done so yet — not completely. I know we traced a laundry mark from her clothes, but there may be a lot of other detail which we — '

'There hasn't been much time for anything like that, Mason, and you know it. Nor has there been much necessity. We'll look around with a toothcomb if we have to. For the moment we're doing exactly as we planned.'

The sergeant said no more. If Royden wanted to be unorthodox he was perfectly entitled to be so. So the enquiry of numerous chemists within the region of the girl's flat commenced and continued without success till towards twelve. On that the two men retired for lunch, then in the early afternoon they were back on the job again — but it was towards four before they had any sign of a break, and then it was at a rather obscure chemists' in a side street.

With a tremendous glow of inner satisfaction Royden found himself looking at the poison book record — and at the very thing he wanted . . . *Janice Elton, 47 Norbury Place, S.W.1.*

'Conclusive?' he asked drily, as Mason stared over his shoulder.

'And in her own name at that,' the sergeant whistled. 'She doesn't seem to have made the slightest effort at hiding it.'

'No . . . she doesn't.' Royden looked pensive for a moment or two, then he crooked a finger at the chemist himself as he stood behind the counter, watching from a distance.

'Yes, Inspector?' He came forward, full of the obvious intention to be of service.

'This is the name I've been looking for,'

Royden explained, his finger on the book. 'Janice — '

'Oh, yes!' The chemist seemed to remember something. 'Wasn't a girl of that name murdered and thrown from a train not so long ago? I seem to remember reading about it.'

'This was *the* girl,' Royden said. 'I'm making a few inquiries in regard to her, as I told you. Now, can you remember what she looked like?'

'Well now, it's rather a long time — '

'Think, man, *think*. It's extremely important.'

The chemist pondered for a while, then a flash of remembrance seemed to cross his face. He snapped his fingers abruptly.

'Of course! She was a blonde, fairly tall, had a languid way of speaking. Yes, I remember her.'

'That's the girl,' Royden nodded, and the chemist looked surprised.

'But why do you need to ask *me* when you know what she looks like?'

'I'm just making sure that we're talking about the same woman. All right, I'm satisfied on that. Now — this is important. Did she give a reason for wanting strychnine?'

'Er — yes she did, as a matter of fact. She said she had to have it because of her physical condition. I didn't inquire as to the full details. After all, it isn't illegal to sell strychnine. It's used for a variety of things.'

'True enough,' Royden agreed, closing the book in front of him. 'Well, thanks very much, sir, for your cooperation. You've told me all I wanted to know.'

'A pleasure, Inspector!'

Royden jerked his head to Mason and left the shop. In the car once more the Inspector summed up.

'Interesting,' he said. 'Yet also puzzling in another way. We have now the curious fact that the murdered girl bought strychnine *herself*, and yet she was murdered with it. On the one hand I could believe that she intended to commit suicide, but on the other hand dead girls are not in the habit of throwing themselves from trains.' Royden shook his head slowly. 'No, it was murder all right — and the only likely suspects at the moment seem to be Martin Lee, who is beyond our reach anyway, and Morgan Dale.'

'Well, she certainly didn't try any trickery in buying the stuff,' Mason said. 'I mean, no false name or anything like that.'

Royden didn't seem to be listening. He was seated with finger and thumb pinched to his eyes. 'The thing that puzzles me is why the bottle has no label on it. The container says it's strychnine, but it ought to be on the bottle as well . . .

'And Lee had the bottle of poison on him, in its carton,' he muttered. 'It's very unlikely he was coming to confess to murder, so what the devil *did* he intend to do? The only theoretical possibility is that he intended to indict Dale as the murderer, and somehow he had got hold of the bottle from Dale. Damn me, this gets more tangled as it goes on.'

'Look here, sir, I've got an idea. Interested to hear it?' Mason looked hopefully at his superior's face.

'Of course I'm interested. Even if your

idea's no good there's no harm in airing it. Let's have it.'

'Well, if Janice Elton *did* need the strychnine for her physical condition she'd perhaps take it with her everywhere she went, wouldn't she?'

'Presumably — yes. Even on the Scots Express.'

'Well, then, it seems to me we've got a good chance of finding out whether suicide was intended or not. We ought to contact her doctor and discover if strychnine was prescribed for her. If it wasn't, then we can consider the idea that she intended to commit suicide — maybe on the train.'

'Mmmm. And then threw herself out of the window?'

'She'd have time to jump after taking the poison. It wouldn't act in the physiological instant of her taking it.'

'And shut the train door after she'd jumped? Remember we have no report of the door ever having been found open. Certainly it was closed — all of them were — when the train came into Glasgow. The porters have said as much.'

Mason shrugged. 'Well, it's just an idea.'

'And perhaps worth following up,' Royden answered, somewhat to the sergeant's surprise. 'We'll have a thorough look at her flat, Mason, and try and find the name of her doctor from there. It's about time we made a complete search of her effects anyway, even as you pointed out this morning . . . Okay, get back to the Yard first and we'll turn this hairbrush into Dabs, then we'll go on to the girl's flat.'

Mason nodded and switched on the ignition. In a matter of twenty minutes their call at the Yard had been completed and Mason was drawing up in the wide forecourt of Norbury Place where stood the ultra-modern building in which the girl's flat was situated.

The flat itself was on the fourth floor, watched over by a constable. He and a second constable had been on duty in shifts ever since the girl's address had been traced. He saluted as Royden and the sergeant came up on to the landing.

'Everything okay, constable?' Royden asked.

'Yes, sir.' The constable opened the

door. 'Nothing's happened, and nobody's been. I rather wish they would. It gets kind of lonely stuck here.'

'One of the joys of the force, my lad.'

Royden preceded Mason into the flat and then glanced about him. He was familiar enough with it from his earlier visitation — the highly modern but rather sparse furniture, the deeply coloured drapes, the soft carpet. Plainly, Janice Elton had used what money she had made to good effect. Everywhere there were little feminine touches, which stamped the place as a woman's.

'We'd better start with the bureau,' Royden said, and pulled at the hinged flap on its front. To his surprise it was not locked. He had fully expected having to use his master key.

'Come to think of it,' Mason said, as Royden lowered the bureau's front and stared inside, 'we haven't come across any keys in Janice's effects. Wonder why? Not even the key to her flat. We had to apply to the agents to get in, if you remember?'

'Yes — I remember.' Royden was gazing at the pigeonholes facing him and the mass of papers in complete untidiness in the main area of the bureau.

'Want me particularly?' Mason asked. 'If you don't I'll prowl around and see if I can find anything interesting.'

'Go ahead,' Royden said, and began to study the papers in front of him, discarding what were obviously bills — paid and unpaid, whilst Mason for his part prowled into the odd corners, looking at this and that, opening drawers and studying the contents thereof.

'Mmm, this is interesting,' Royden said, after about ten minutes of investigative silence amongst the papers.

Mason glanced at him and came over. 'What, sir?'

'This letter. Listen — 'Dearest Janice, I am afraid that the demands you make of me cannot be met any longer, and for both our sakes it would be as well if you do not attempt anything further, otherwise I shall be compelled to take stronger action. Sorry, but I know you'll understand. Morgan'.'

Mason took the letter as the Chief-Inspector held it out to him. He frowned over it.

'Sounds as though Dale had more to do with Janice than he makes out, sir.'

Royden did not answer. He was studying something else — a further letter. Both this one and the other one had been in a pigeonhole by themselves, well separated from the general disorder in the body of the bureau.

'Decidedly interesting,' Royden commented. 'Listen again, sergeant — 'Dearest Janice, Your request for something like seven thousand pounds is quite out of all reason, and despite the lever you imagine you have against me I'll risk your using it. Morgan'.'

'Blackmail perhaps?' Mason suggested, taking the second letter and looking at it.

'Perhaps,' Royden assented, thinking. 'At least that's the impression intended to be conveyed.'

'Surely it *is* conveyed. No doubt about it. These letters, typewritten — and signed by Dale himself. I'm not conversant with his signature but we can soon check it.'

'There's something odd about it,' Royden said. 'For one thing these two letters were stuck in a pigeonhole where we couldn't help but notice them. For another, the bureau was unlocked . . . In a word, nothing to stop anybody looking in it any time they wanted to, or to put it more pointedly — no hindrance whatever for the police or anybody else to look at the letters.'

'You mean you think it's a plant on Janice's part?'

'That's certainly a possibility and I'll carry it in mind. We'll take those letters and confront Dale with them at the right moment . . . Now, who the dickens is the girl's doctor?'

Royden commenced another search. Mason folded the two letters that had been found, put them in an envelope, and then in his wallet. After that he watched Royden continuing his search, then he set off on further investigation on his own account. And to a certain extent, some time afterwards, it was an investigation that yielded fruit. In one of the girl's coats hanging in the wardrobe he discovered a bunch of keys. Promptly he came back to Royden with them.

'This looks like the bunch of keys we've

been wondering about, sir,' Mason said. 'We didn't examine the clothes in the wardrobe very thoroughly in the first look round.'

Royden glanced up from studying a small, hard-backed address book.

'Where were they, anyhow?'

'In an overcoat.' Mason headed for the door. 'I'll just check this Yale.'

He did, satisfied himself it was indeed the key to the flat, and then came back to the chief Inspector's side.

'That settles that, sir. There are four others as you see. We'll probably find out in due course what they're for.'

'Mmm. Hang on to them, Mason: they'll go in the locker along with the letters . . . Y'know, it's odd that Janice should decide to go on a journey to Scotland without taking her keys. She doesn't seem to have had a handbag, either. Why did she travel so light?'

'No idea, sir.'

'Well, I have. Maybe she never intended coming back anyway.'

Mason thought this out for a moment but he did not have time to form any conclusion for Royden went on:

'I've found the address of a doctor in this book here. I don't know if he's the one who's been attending Janice but at least it's worth a try. We'd better go and have a word with him. Come on.'

Mason nodded and followed his superior from the flat. In a space of fifteen minutes they were at the house named in the address book Royden was carrying with him and a trim receptionist showed the two men into a waiting room.

Presently the M.D. appeared, a tall eagle of a man in a white overall.

'Good afternoon, gentlemen . . . ' He paused, looking from one to the other through horn-rimmed glasses. 'These are not really surgery hours, you know — '

'We're not patients, doctor. I'm a police officer.' Royden exhibited his warrant-card. 'It's possible you can give me some information.'

'Gladly. What can I do?'

'Was a Miss Janice Elton one of your patients?'

'Er — Janice Elton?' The M.D. reflected swiftly and then nodded. 'Yes, of course she is. But,' — he seemed puzzled — 'you said *was?*'

'Miss Elton is dead, doctor. Has been for some time. If you read the newspapers you'd know the facts. The theory is that she was murdered.'

'Good Lord, how shocking! And you? Since you're from the police you presumably wish to know something about her?'

'Only one thing, doctor. I believe you were treating her for a fatal disease — leukaemia to be exact?'

'I was, yes.'

'Did, you at any time prescribe strychnine for her condition?'

'Strychnine?' The M.D. looked astonished, 'Certainly not. As a matter of fact that would be the last thing I'd do.'

'I see. And were you the only doctor Miss Elton consulted?'

'I believe she had an examination by Dr. Thornton at the City and General Hospital, but that was on my advice considering the disease she was suffering from.'

Royden nodded. 'And if anybody prescribed strychnine it would be Dr. Thornton, I take it?'

'Yes, but — ' The M.D. shook his head. 'For the life of me I can't think why strychnine should be suggested. It just doesn't fit the case.'

The Chief-Inspector smiled. 'All right, doctor. Thanks for your help. We'll contact Dr. Thornton, and see what he has to say.'

'Would I be trespassing if I asked what strychnine has got to do with it? You spoke of murder, and — I'm in a bit of a fog.'

'I am endeavouring to sort out the problem of the strychnine which killed Janice Elton,' Royden shrugged. 'So far I've found out that she obtained it under the pretext of it being for her physical condition.'

'Hardly a pretext surely? Anybody can buy strychnine if they sign the poison book.'

'Well, then, let's say she added the information of her own volition. You can see why I wanted to check on it . . . '

'Of course — of course. Anyway, perhaps Dr. Thornton will be able to give you a fresh slant on the matter . . . '

But in this hope the M.D. was wrong. Dr. Thornton also denied the possibility of strychnine being necessary for leukaemia, with the result that two rather puzzled men landed back eventually at Scotland Yard in the early evening.

'So far, so bad,' Mason commented, rather gloomily. 'What do we do now? Pack it up for the day or shall I get some sandwiches and tea?'

'Get sandwiches and tea. We've something to talk out before we finish for the day.'

'Right, sir.'

Mason left the office and Royden turned to his desk and considered the various items of information that had come in during the day for his attention. One memorandum said that the driver of the car which had ultimately killed Martin Lee had been found and charged with manslaughter — but the most important information, from Royden's point of view, was the fingerprint report No. 2 from Dabs, using Martin Lee's hairbrush for specimen prints.

Royden read it carefully:

Further report on poison bottle and container reference Janice Elton deceased.

From specimen prints submitted on hairbrush (returned herewith) it is obvious that there are distinct prints of Martin Lee's both on poison bottle and container. This is in addition to the prints mentioned in earlier report No. 1.

Royden read the report through again, considered it, and then handed it to Mason to read when he came back with the tea and sandwiches. The Sergeant rubbed the back of his head in vague perplexity.

'Looks to me, sir, as though we're forced into the conclusion that Lee did the job after all. With all his prints on the bottle and container what else are we to think?'

Royden said: 'Don't forget that Dale's prints are on the bottle as well, so he also had hold of it at some time. The point here is that he's alive and can be questioned, or even tricked into admitting something. Lee can't.'

'Might have been a job handled by both men,' Mason suggested, reaching to a sandwich.

'With the girl herself buying the poison,' Royden sighed. 'It's the queerest business ever. She bought the poison for a specific *purpose*. The red herring about her needing it for a physical condition we can forget since the medicos have disproved it. She leaves her flat, leaves her keys, and also leaves two condemnatory letters, which were not difficult to find — just as though she intended killing herself on the train to Scotland and leaving letters behind to suggest that she had been *murdered*.'

'Suppose,' Mason said, drinking some tea, 'it was suicide on Janice's part and that either Lee or Dale — or both of them — discovered her suicide and tipped her out of the window to avoid being implicated in what might look like murder?'

Such is the way of life, Sergeant Mason had given the right answer in an inspired moment — but the Chief-Inspector didn't look particularly impressed.

'That theory is too simple, Mason — and it has too many holes in it as well. I don't think they'd throw a suicide off the train for fear of being implicated in the suggestion of murder. Of course, they *might*, but — No, no, it doesn't fit somehow. Then again, that doesn't fit in with the fact that Lee was anxious to see me at the Yard, carrying a bottle — *the* bottle — with his own and Dale's prints on it, to say nothing of the girl's. No I still lean to the murder angle even if I don't seem to be getting anywhere at the moment, and I still half believe that Lee was the culprit.'

'But he doesn't seem to have had any earlier connections with Janice, sir. Dale *had*: he even admitted the fact. And then those letters of Janice's — '

'Planted! Planted, I'm convinced.' Royden pulled a cup of tea towards him and drank it whilst he worried out the details in his mind.

'With Lee apparently involved in this business as much as he is, wouldn't it be a good idea to investigate his background?' Mason suggested presently. 'I know he's dead and can never be convicted, but at least it would perhaps convince us as to where the blame lies. If there's no clue, then turn the pressure on Dale. It's a toss-up between him and Lee now.'

'True enough . . . ' Royden shifted uncomfortably in his chair. 'There are such a lot of bits and pieces in this matter. They don't fit in. For instance, Janice had no handbag that we could find, no trace of a ticket for her train journey — No money, and no poison bottle. The *bottle* turns up with Lee, who gets killed before he can explain. Somehow he must have got it from Janice . . . Right! We'll find out from his widow as much as we can when we return this hairbrush. Maybe we'd better go tonight, then we shan't be involved in the funeral arrangements tomorrow.'

'As you say, sir,' Mason agreed, and mentally wondered why he had ever got involved in such a crazy business as the police force. He ate another sandwich and sighed over the evening at his drama group, which he would be quite unable to attend.

So, towards seven-thirty, the two men arrived at the late Martin Lee's home and once again saw his impassive and decidedly indifferent wife. She ushered them into the lounge and then looked at them enquiringly.

'The hairbrush, Madam,' Royden said quietly, handing it back to her in the cellophane envelope. 'It has been most useful to us in proving certain points.'

'I'm glad,' Mrs. Lee said — and waited.

'I have also to inform you that the man responsible for the accident which caused your husband's death has been apprehended and charged with manslaughter. The case will come up in a very short time when the matter of compensation will also be decided.'

'I understand.'

'Now to something else. I'm afraid you'll have to know about it, Mrs. Lee, sooner or later — so it may as well be now, and I apologize for bringing up unpleasantness at a time like this.'

Mrs. Lee laughed shortly. 'There's no need for apologies, Inspector. I may as well tell you that I'm not half so grief stricken as perhaps I ought to be. Martin and I were not exactly — ideally suited to each other. Though I regret the tragic nature of his death I feel for the first time in my married life a great sense of freedom. You understand?'

'Yes, I think so,' Royden agreed quietly.

'Martin was a milk-and-water clerk in business and a despot at home,' Mrs. Lee elaborated. 'He was a — Oh, well, never mind. Let the dead rest. What was the unpleasantness you wished to mention, Inspector?'

The chief Inspector asked a question: 'Did Mr. Lee ever mention a Janice Elton, Mrs. Lee?'

'Oh, yes — quite frequently. She used to be a personal secretary to Mr. Dale, and then got the sack for her rather unwelcome affectionate advances, or something. Since then she's been murdered and — ' Mrs. Lee hesitated. 'But why do I need to tell you all this? You must know, of course.'

'Of course,' Royden assented. 'I'm handling the case of her murder, and by a combination of circumstances your late husband comes into the business . . . How well did he know Janice Elton? Can you tell me that?'

'As far as I know he only knew her as a business associate. Frankly, I don't think there was anything more. Whatever else my husband may have been he was not a ladies' man. He never gave me any worries on that score.'

'I see. Can you tell me, then, how he stood with Mr. Dale? Was he a trusted employee — ?'

'Most trusted. He'd been with Mr. Dale for over twenty years.'

'Mmm. A sort of right hand man in fact?'

'Yes.' Mrs. Lee looked vaguely surprised. 'That's just what Martin used to call himself. The very words! Funny you should use them. But tell me, Inspector, where is all this leading? What do you want to know so much about Martin for?'

'I'm afraid it's vital that I should. You are aware from the newspapers perhaps that Janice Elton was murdered by poison — strychnine?'

'Yes. I noticed that.'

'Well, here's something you won't know because we haven't publicised it. Your husband was coming to see me at Scotland Yard when he met with that accident, and in his pocket was an empty poison bottle which has since been proven to have strychnine in it.'

Mrs. Lee stared. 'But — but good heavens, you don't think Martin could have poisoned Janice, do you? It's out of the question! He wasn't that type. Wouldn't have the nerve.'

'In my position, madam, I wouldn't be foolish enough to suggest that such and such a person committed murder without being absolutely sure of my facts. I'm not suggesting anything with regard to your late husband, but the coincidence of the poison bottle definitely intrigues me and I want to find out more about it. Your husband didn't mention to you, I suppose, that he was going to call upon Scotland Yard?'

'Gracious, no! He never mentioned such a thing.'

'Which leaves us with two alternatives. Either he never intended to say anything to you, or else he made the decision suddenly — perhaps at lunchtime.'

'Why lunchtime particularly? He came home to his lunch every day, including the day he was killed. He never said a word.'

'And you've never seen him handling a poison bottle or anything whilst he was at home?'

'Never. Of course he might have kept anything like that hidden. He had ample opportunity to hide anything he brought in — I mean that big briefcase of his. I've never known what was in it, and I haven't particularly cared either.'

'Briefcase?' Royden repeated.

'I haven't seen it since he was killed. I suppose it's at the office. He went out with it as usual on the day he was killed, but evidently he hadn't it with him when he met with the accident.'

The Chief-Inspector reflected for a moment then changed his line of conversation. He asked a question.

'With whom did your husband make friends, Mrs. Lee? Anybody connected with Janice Elton?'

'Not as far as I know. Martin didn't make friends easily, and he kept himself to himself most of the time. His main interests seemed to be in doing things about the house and garden — Just lately he was very active in that direction, making preparations for our removal. Unfortunately I don't think things will come off as we intended in that direction. I hardly feel like taking on a five thousand pound house just for myself.'

Royden raised his eyebrows. 'Forgive me mentioning it, Mrs. Lee, but a house of that value is a bit out of the scope of a chief clerk, isn't it? In the ordinary way, I mean. Or perhaps you're referring to an investment of your own, or a legacy maybe — '

'I'm referring,' Mrs. Lee said deliberately, 'to the only sensible thing Martin ever did in his life. For years I've been nagging him about this house — which isn't particularly marvellous as you can see — and my continued grumbling must have impressed him for about three weeks ago Martin raised a loan of five thousand pounds from Mr. Dale and bought a new house with it. Don't ask me how the miracle happened, but it did.'

'Very interesting,' Royden said, with a glance at Mason. 'And everything was all set for this new house when your husband was killed? Most unfortunate for you.'

Mrs. Lee nodded self-piteously. 'So I think — particularly as Martin seemed at last to have turned the financial corner. He told me after buying the house that there'd be plenty of money coming in any time he wanted it.'

'Did he now?' Royden pondered for a moment. 'And this sudden acquisition of money was about three weeks ago, you say?'

'Three weeks or a fortnight. I don't quite remember really.'

Royden smiled. 'No; that's hardly to be expected when so many disturbing things have been happening to you recently . . . Well, Mrs. Lee, I won't take up any more of your time. Let's be on our way, Mason.'

The two men took their leave, but Mason only drove into the next street then at Royden's request he stopped again.

'I just want to think while I've got

everything clear in my mind,' the Chief-Inspector said. 'In my view, two interesting things have emerged from that interview — '

'Yes, sir. The five thousand pounds and the briefcase. Right?'

'Right! The briefcase isn't vital but it might be worth taking a look at — so we'll call on Dale tomorrow and have him give it to us. There may be something in it which will provide a clue, however slight.'

'Which Dale will have removed by this time.'

'Possibly, yes — but we'll have a look just the same. Anyway, the most significant thing yet is that five thousand pound house provided by Dale. Men like him don't part with that kind of money to a chief clerk without a very good reason. *And* there's the other point that Lee said to his wife there was plenty more money where that came from. You thinking what I'm thinking, sergeant?'

'Yes, sir. Blackmail!'

6

Dale Changes His Story

It was towards mid-morning on the following day when Royden and Mason were shown into Dale's office. He greeted them cordially enough even though he wondered inwardly what was coming next. He had fully expected they would appear again before long, but he had hardly expected them quite so soon.

'Well?' he asked quietly, when they had seated themselves. 'What now, gentlemen?'

'First — this,' the chief Inspector said, and took from his briefcase the two letters which he had obtained from Janice Elton's flat. He handed them over and waited, watching intently.

'Utterly fantastic nonsense!' he declared finally. 'They're forgeries, down to the signature. That's a reasonable copy of my signature, but that's all. I don't know anything about them. Where did you get them?'

'Janice Elton's flat.' Royden put them back in his briefcase. 'All right, sir, you say they are forgeries — '

'Certainly they are, typed by Janice herself I suppose. She could easily copy my signature. She used to see it a hundred times a day on the various letters she handled.'

'Have you any suggestions as to why she should do such a thing?'

Dale passed a hand over his bald pate and made a worried movement. 'Spite, I should think. Or maybe she knew she was going to be murdered, or something, and wanted to make it seem that I'd had something to do with it. *I* don't know. I've told you already how much she hated me because I repulsed her amorous advances . . . Anyway, I disclaim all knowledge of those letters and you can place on them what construction you like.'

'Thank you for the privilege,' Royden murmured dryly. 'Well, Mr. Dale, let's take another aspect — and I'll not beat about the bush concerning it . . . Here it is: how did you come to give Martin Lee five thousand pounds to buy a new house?'

Dale looked at the blotter on his desk before he answered slowly, 'I did it because I thought he was entitled to a bonus after twenty years of hard work. I've never given him anything really worthwhile and so — Well, I felt generous, having just pulled off a big deal with Lee's help I felt it was a way of showing my appreciation.'

'Oh,' Royden said — and nothing else. Dale looked up in surprise.

'There was nothing wrong in what I did, surely?'

'Nothing wrong, sir — no. It just seems an unusual thing to do. How would you suggest that ties up with Lee remarking to his wife that there was plenty more money where that five thousand had come from?'

'You've been talking to her then?'

'Obviously.' Royden's expression changed. 'And I'll tell you this much. Mr. Dale: I don't believe a word of your story about giving Lee a bonus. Businessmen just *don't* give away five thousand pounds like that without a reasonable security. I suggest that Lee was blackmailing you, for some reason or other.'

'Nonsense.' Dale gave a gusty laugh. 'What on earth should he want to blackmail me for?'

'Suppose you tell *me*, sir? Why otherwise did Lee anticipate getting all the money he wanted, and presumably from the same source?'

'I've no idea what he was talking about.'

'I have — and I think Janice Elton is mixed up with it.'

Dale shrugged, tautly calm. 'All right, Inspector. I can't stop you thinking, can I?'

'I suggest that Lee knew you and Janice Elton had been closely connected in some way. He got the poison bottle from you — how I don't know yet — and came to the Yard with it intending to tell me something about it, but he was killed before he could do anything . . . For your information, Mr. Dale, your fingerprints are clearly visible on the poison bottle, together with Lee's and the girl's. You must have had hold of it at some time.'

Dale shrugged. 'Maybe — but I honestly don't recall when it could have been.'

'Come, come, Mr. Dale, you can do

better than that!' Royden was smiling icily. 'One does not take hold of a poison bottle and then forget all about it. Not in a case like this with a girl murdered as the issue.'

Dale was silent, meditating. In fact he was meditating on quite a few things — chiefly the alarming rate at which the Inspector seemed to be catching up on everything, Finally he said:

'Yes, I remember now. Lee handed me that bottle in this very office a few days ago. But he didn't say it had had strychnine in it. He simply asked me what it was doing in his office.'

'In his office? I don't quite follow.'

'Neither did I at the time, but it seemed that he had been cleaning the place up a bit. In the course of doing so he came across the bottle in one of the drawers and brought it in to me, asking if I knew anything about it. Naturally, I took it in my hand to examine it.'

The Inspector shrugged. 'So that's your explanation, is it?'

'Certainly it is — and it's the correct one.'

Royden did not pursue the subject. Instead he asked another question:

'Martin Lee had a briefcase, I believe, which he usually took home with him at night. I understand it is in his office, and has been since the day he died. If you don't mind I'll take it along with me to the Yard.'

'I'm hardly in a position to stop you, am I?' Dale asked grimly. 'As a matter of fact I don't know whether the case is there or not: I haven't looked in Lee's office very thoroughly since he died. Anyway, we can soon settle it.'

He got to his feet, opened the door, and led the way down the short corridor to another glass-panelled door inscribed *Martin Lee, Chief Clerk*. He opened the door with a key and then stood aside for the Inspector and Mason to enter.

'Just as Lee left it, more or less,' Dale said. 'I've been in to rescue certain important papers, but that's all. Ah! There's the briefcase — by the filing cabinet there.'

Mason picked it up and then glanced at his superior. Royden gave a satisfied nod and turned again to Dale.

'I think that will be all for the time being, Mr. Dale,' he said. 'Naturally our enquiry will continue and if I need to speak to you again I know where to contact you.'

Dale nodded his bald head. 'Of course, Inspector.'

Royden paused for a moment as he was about to pass through the office doorway. His rapier eyes looked at Dale squarely.

'I wonder if you'd do me a favour, Mr. Dale?'

'Of course — if I can.'

'All right then. Next time I see you, try and think up a better story to explain the poison bottle away. Your fingerprints are indisputable, you know, and the idea of Lee finding the bottle in this office whilst cleaning it out is, frankly, completely unconvincing. Okay?'

'I tell you it's the truth,' Dale snapped.

Royden smiled. 'All right, if you *must* try and confuse the issue let it go at that. I'm afraid you may be sorry later. Coming, Mason?'

The sergeant went out quietly. Dale

stood watching the two men stride along the landing and disappear down the staircase, then he closed Lee's office door slowly and pondered to himself.

'Why the devil do they want that briefcase anyway?' he muttered. 'It's caught me on the hop has that. And I never even thought of examining it first . . . '

He went back slowly to his own office, lost in a maze of troubled thoughts — and meanwhile Royden and Mason had reached the police car. For once, Royden did not hold an impromptu conference: he briefly instructed Mason to return to the Yard, and spent the short journey with Lee's briefcase on his knees and a faraway look in his eyes.

Not until he was in his office again did he unburden himself.

'I can't make head or tail of Dale,' he said frankly, unfastening Lee's briefcase. 'Deep down inside me there's a conviction that he's on the square — that he's a cagey victim of circumstances, but on the other hand he doesn't do anything to inspire my confidence. Did you ever hear such a cock-and-bull story as that one he gave about the poison bottle? Good Lord, it wouldn't convince a child!'

'Maybe his reaction is that of a very frightened man?' Mason suggested. 'He's scared to give the real facts and so invents all sorts of excuses. It wouldn't be the first time a suspect has reacted in that fashion.'

'No; and maybe you're right . . . ' Royden pulled away the second strap of Lee's briefcase. 'Anyhow, I'm quite sure that he didn't write those letters we found in Janice's flat. It wasn't even worth checking Dale's signature. She planted those herself, and she evidently didn't give the police credit for having much analytical power . . . That's what I mean when I say I think Dale is the victim of circumstances and afraid to tell the truth . . . '

With a sudden jerk Royden unfastened the clasp of the briefcase and pulled back the flap. He turned the entire case upside down and tipped out several sheets of calculations, a book on economics, a couple of pencils, and a business sales graph.

'Not very hopeful,' Mason said, surveying the turnout.

126

'I hardly expected it would be, but you never know until you try,' Royden said. 'There might have been some clue as to his connection — if any — with Janice Elton, but it seems that we — ' Royden stopped, sniffing vigorously. Then finally he sniffed inside the briefcase.

'What?' Mason asked curiously.

'I don't quite know. There's a faint perfume in this case. Here — smell for yourself. My sniffing powers are a bit blunted through smoking a lot.'

Mason did as he was ordered, thought for a moment, then gave a confirmatory nod.

'Smells rather like lilac,' he said.

'Lee wasn't that kind of man, I'm sure,' the Chief-Inspector said. 'In fact I'd say he'd scorn any perfume of any kind, and there was certainly no smell of perfume about the clothes he was wearing when he met his death.'

Silence for a moment, then Mason snapped his fingers.

'Wait a minute, sir! I've smelled something like that before — and not so long ago. I remember now: it was yesterday when I was searching through Janice's wardrobe. Her clothes carried a perfume like that about them.'

'The devil they did! Here, wait a minute — '

Royden turned to one of the big lockers bearing a label with Janice Elton's name upon it. He opened it and pulled forth a plastic bag in which lay the mustard suit in which she had died. Opening the bag's top he sniffed inside it — then he smiled. Very faintly an aroma reached him, identical with that from the briefcase.

'Mmm, so we're off on another tack,' he said, resealing the mustard-coloured suit and returning it to the locker. 'The perfume is Janice's — not very strong on this suit because of the time she was in the open air. In fact it's probably only the enclosure of the plastic bag that causes any perfume at all to be detectable. The briefcase being closed up has also caused perfume to linger — but how on earth did the aroma get in there in the first place?'

'That's a bit of a puzzle, sir. Lee evidently carried something of Janice's in this case, but I can't imagine what. Hardly an article of clothing, surely?'

'No, that doesn't seem to tie up,' Royden said, musing. 'But I know something that *does*! Her *handbag* — one of the items that has been missing since the start. If anything retains the aroma of perfume it's a handbag, because it is almost continually closed up. I know that much from my wife's bag.'

'Looks as though you may have hit it, sir. Perhaps, even, there was a satchet of this perfume or something in the bag, which caused the aroma to be noticeable. Noticeable enough to leave traces in this briefcase, anyway.'

'Which raises a point,' Royden said. 'What was Janice's handbag doing in Lee's briefcase?' He thought for a moment and then shrugged. 'Anyway, we can skip that part of the business, the main thing we know is that Lee certainly must have had a connection with Janice, which rather eases the strain somewhat on Morgan Dale.'

'There's another angle too,' Mason commented.

'Well?'

'This briefcase has been in Dale's reach

for some time since Lee died. How do we know it was *Lee* who caused the perfume odour to be there? Dale, if he wanted to shift the focus of suspicion, might have deliberately caused this perfume to be present. Always assuming, that is, that he knew Janice used a perfume like this. And he very probably *would* know since she worked side by side with him for a long time. Of course, he didn't know we were going to take the briefcase but he might have had a good idea that we would.'

Royden said slowly: 'It might be a good idea to find out if this perfume is a fairly common brand. If so, Lee might have got it from something of his wife's, seeing that he took his briefcase home quite a lot. We don't *know* the aroma is that of Janice's exclusively. If it is a commonly used perfume Mrs. Lee might have used it also. We've got to be sure about it. I think we'd better hop along to Janice's flat and see if there's any of this perfume in the place. Let's go.'

They were at Janice's guarded flat in a matter of minutes, but even so their search was a fruitless one. Amongst the variety of cosmetics, which Janice had been in the habit of using there was no sign of a bottle containing the perfume required.

'Well,' Royden said finally, inspecting a bottle of nail varnish, 'there's one other lead we can try. On several of these cosmetic bottles, even though they're well-known brands, there's also the labelled imprint of a well-known beauty salon in Chandos Street. See?'

Mason looked at the superimposed label with its gold lettering and nodded.

'Since Chandos Street is only round the corner it's a reasonable assumption that Janice bought all her cosmetics, including the elusive perfume, from there. Might be worth finding out.'

'Yes, sir,' Mason agreed, rather uneasily.

Royden put down the bottle of nail varnish and stared. 'What's worrying you, Mason?'

'Er — nothing sir. I suppose you'll want me to accompany you?'

'I most certainly will. You don't think I'm going into that lionesses' den alone, do you? All right, so you'll feel embarrassed. That makes two of us — but it's got to be done just the same.'

'How do we describe the perfume, sir?'

'We don't. We'll slip back to the Yard and get the briefcase. Come on.'

Some twenty minutes later they were entering the glass and chromium doors of Maison Cherise, distinctly unfamiliar ground for them — and tough though they were in the ordinary way they certainly did not feel safe. Feeling very much like mortal sinners in the abode of saints they crossed over the soundless pile carpet to a little horseshoe shaped table where a receptionist watched their advance with aloof interest.

'Might I see the proprietress?' Royden asked, raising his hat.

'I'm sorry, sir, but I'm afraid that isn't possible. She's away in Paris at the moment.'

'Oh . . . ' Royden juggled with the setback and the tall girl in the form-fitting black dress surveyed him with polite interest. Presently her heavily made-up eyes dropped to the briefcase he was carrying.

'If you are a traveller, sir — '

'No — anything but that.' Royden produced his warrant card. 'This explains who I am, and perhaps you can help me. I am trying to trace a particular brand of perfume.'

'I'll be glad to help you if I can, Inspector.' It was surprising how the girl had thawed. 'What particular brand of perfume are you referring to?'

'This.' The Chief-Inspector opened the briefcase and held back the flap. 'I can't describe it. It would be better if you smelled it for yourself.'

The girl twitched delicate nostrils over the briefcase, thought for a moment, then sniffed again. Finally something seemed to occur to her.

'I believe it's lilac essence. Just a moment.' She turned away, examined the brilliantly-lighted glass counters nearby, then presently returned with something that looked like a small pocket book. She opened it and, surprisingly, sniffed at it.

'Yes,' she confirmed. 'That's it. Smell for yourself.'

Both Royden and Mason sniffed at the

leaves of the book the girl had brought. There was no doubt about it: it was the identical perfume.

'Then it isn't actually a perfume in a bottle?' Royden asked.

'No, Inspector. It only exists in this form. There are a hundred leaves in this book, each one perforated. They can be torn out, wiped on the face and hands, and so remove grime and dust. They're wipe-aways, really.'

'Mmm, I see. The kind of thing a girl might carry in her handbag, for instance?'

'I should think it highly probable.'

'And are these — er — refresher leaves in common use? That is, could they be bought almost anywhere?'

The girl looked vaguely offended. 'Most certainly not. They are exclusive to Maison Cherise.'

The Chief-Inspector smiled and fastened the briefcase up again.

'Thank you so much, miss. That's all I wanted to know.'

Feeling like a man who has walked the plank Royden led the way out of the salon again, Mason beside him. They didn't breathe freely until they were back in the car.

'Thank goodness that's over!' Mason blew out his cheeks expressively. 'There are some parts of a policeman's lot which I don't like at all, sir.'

'I couldn't agree more. However — to business. I think we can take it as certain that the perfume in this briefcase is — or rather was — Janice's, which came originally from her handbag. It's too unlikely that Mrs. Lee is the cause. I don't think she'd be likely to visit Maison Cherise when she lives so far away from it. Okay, so Lee had much closer connections with Janice than we at first thought — close enough for him to put her handbag in his briefcase.'

'Suppose,' Mason said, 'we make a search of Lee's home and try and unearth something that might show conclusively what the connection was between Lee and Janice? On the face of things it begins to look more and more as though he murdered her — and that Dale's prints on the poison bottle are merely secondary. You never know, he might even have been speaking the truth when he said Lee found the bottle while cleaning his office out.'

'Truth my foot!' Royden gave a snort. 'There's some other answer to that — just as there's an answer to the mystery of why Lee tried to see me separately from Dale ... Y'know, we've both said that Dale's *hiding* something, and we've got to find out what it is, otherwise we'll keep on going round in circles. Direct questioning seems to be no use — Dale's too wary for that — so maybe it would be a better idea to have his movements watched and see if he does anything suspicious.'

Mason looked surprised. 'No reason why he should, is there?'

'I dunno. He knows by now that we're suspicious of him, and men who realize the law's watching them do all kinds of odd things, either to prove their guilt or their innocence. I don't see why Dale should be an exception. We can afford to wait for a definite lead ... Right. Get back to the Yard and I'll have a couple of men watch him.'

* * *

Meanwhile, Morgan Dale was doing a good deal of thinking whilst, outwardly, he went about his work in the usual way. Royden had certainly guessed right in saying that Dale knew the law was suspicious of him, and the more he thought about this fact the more worried he became.

'Maybe I was wrong in that excuse about the poison bottle,' he muttered, staring at the desk in front of him. 'Yet on the other hand I couldn't give any other explanation without having time to think. Trouble is, fingerprints don't lie. They're mine — and the police can think what they like about them. If they choose to think the wrong thing about me I'm going to be in the hell of a mess before I'm finished.'

He went through the day turning the business over in his mind, seeking some clear lead as to what he should do next. In this respect, Royden had guessed the psychology of his man quite accurately: the more he was left alone the more Dale built up in his mind a picture of what he imagined was happening behind the scenes — so much so that, by evening, Dale had arrived at a decision. Janice and Lee were both dead and could never speak. Why not pin the blame on Lee and build everything up to show *he* was the murderer of Janice? It was no use telling the truth — that Janice had committed suicide — because that left out the problem of explaining how she had fallen from the train.

A picture clear in his mind, Dale left the office earlier than usual and went direct to Scotland Yard. Thanks to the p.c. men whom he had watching Dale, Royden knew that Dale was coming, but nonetheless he effected a convincing surprise as the financier was shown into his office.

'So you come to me for a change, Mr. Dale,' Royden smiled, motioning to a chair. 'What's on your mind?'

'One or two things I think I ought to get straight.' Dale spoke with the air of a man who has come to a firm decision, and over at his corner table Mason unobtrusively drew a notebook to him.

Royden returned to his desk and sat down. He passed over cigarettes and then relaxed, his rapier-keen eyes watching intently, as Dale inhaled nervously.

'Well?' Royden asked at length.

'I have to admit to lying to you this morning, Inspector. About the poison bottle, I mean.'

Royden smiled. 'I know you did. Better give me the real story, hadn't you?'

'That's my present intention. Janice Elton boarded the same train as Lee and myself, but we were not aware of that fact until the journey was nearly over. She came to our compartment and insisted on seeing Lee privately. I didn't take kindly to the idea, of course, but it seemed such an urgent matter I left them together and went out into the corridor. Actually I went into the lavatory and washed my hands. About ten minutes later I came back. Lee whirled me into the compartment and pointed to Janice, She was lying dead on the seat. He also gave me the poison bottle to look at and said he'd dosed her with a large quantity of strychnine.'

'Which explains how your prints got on the bottle?'

'Naturally.'

'Then what happened?'

'We had an argument over the business. I wanted to pull the communication cord but Lee stopped me. In fact he knocked me out for a while by hitting me over the head with something hard. I never found out what it was. When I came to again we were pulling into Glasgow and Lee said he'd thrown the girl's body out of the window.'

'Then he must have been stronger than he looked,' Royden commented. 'To lift a girl of Janice's type, and dead weight at that would be no easy task . . . However, go on.'

Dale felt as though he were on slippery mud. He tried to get a hold on himself and continued:

'Lee threatened what he'd do to me if I dared say he had murdered the girl. I went in fear of what he would do next. I even gave him five thousand pounds when he asked for it. Otherwise I'm sure he would have murdered me. With one murder on his conscience it wouldn't matter how many more he committed, and I knew it. The greatest relief to me was when I learned he had been killed.'

'All of which,' Royden said, 'accounts for the poison bottle being in his possession, I suppose?'

'Naturally.'

'In face of this story, Mr. Dale, why do you think Lee tried to see me at the Yard?'

'I've no idea — unless he wanted by some trickery to implicate me as Janice's murderer.'

'Mmm — could be.' Royden stared at the ceiling. 'It all seems very odd. You see, Janice bought the poison *herself*, and yet it was Lee who used it upon her. How do you account for that?'

'I should have told you, Inspector — Janice tried to poison Lee in the compartment but he turned the tables on her.'

Royden raised his eyebrows. 'Do you mean that the girl was going to try and force strychnine down Lee's throat? Was going to do *that* to a man in full possession of his strength and senses?

141

She'd never have succeeded in a million years.'

'She was . . . slightly unbalanced . . . ' Dale said quietly.

The Chief-Inspector's eyes sharpened. 'What makes you, think so?'

'The way she behaved in the compartment at first. It was queer somehow. Definite mental aberration, I'd say, though I'm not really qualified to judge. Entirely different from the Janice who used to work beside me. Though, come to think of it her amorous regard for me wasn't entirely normal, was it? Yes, I'm sure she was unhinged somewhere . . . '

7

'Fingerprints Don't Lie'

There was a long silence, somehow not at all reassuring to Dale — then with something of an effort he spoke again.

'Perhaps the disease she was suffering from had something to do with her queer behaviour.'

'Perhaps,' Royden agreed, 'though it's hardly likely. I never heard of leukaemia making a person mental . . . Anyway, this is all very interesting, Mr. Dale, even though it doesn't explain why Lee should hate Janice enough to want to kill her.'

Dale shrugged. 'I don't think he *did* hate her actually, unless there was something between them that I've never known about. I tell you — Janice tried to kill Lee, but he turned the tables and killed her instead.'

Royden smiled enigmatically. 'Tell me, Mr. Dale, do you know what kind of perfume Janice used to wear?'

'Perfume?' The financier looked surprised. 'Why, no. I haven't any idea.'

'You never detected a perfume when she was beside you?'

'Not that I remember. Certainly nothing worth remembering. Why?'

'Oh, just a thought,' Royden said vaguely; then he returned directly to the matter on hand. 'From your story it seems pretty certain Lee caused Janice's death, but there are still one or two odds and ends that want fitting in.'

'For instance?'

'Janice's handbag, for one thing. She would surely carry one, and it hasn't been found. Maybe you know what Lee did with it?'

Dale thought. 'I don't really know. In fact I don't remember seeing it.'

'Oh, I think she would certainly have had it with her,' Royden said. 'Our enquiry has revealed that it wasn't found anywhere on the train — and in any case I don't think for a moment that she'd leave it in her own compartment. Surely it would contain her railway ticket, money, and the usual odds and ends. Yes, even the bottle of poison.'

'She might have carried that in her suit pocket,' Dale suggested.

'Not very likely. It hasn't any real pockets — only false ones that are nothing more than slits in the cloth. No, she'd have her bag all right.'

Silence. Dale looked at the papers on the desk, aware as he did so of Royden's calm, unrelenting scrutiny.

'I've been wondering about something . . . ' Dale said at last.

'For instance?'

'About this handbag business. I've never mentioned it before — in fact I'd forgotten all about it — but somebody burned something in my office grate a little while after Janice was murdered.'

Royden's eyes sharpened. 'Burned something?'

'I don't know what exactly: it must have been done during the night when I was away. When *everybody* was away, in fact. I couldn't find out who'd done it. All I could discover was a pile of brown, cardboardy ash as though somebody had burned a carton or something. I didn't inquire too thoroughly at the time because it didn't seem too significant a matter — but now I'm commencing to wonder. Since Lee killed Janice and somehow hid the handbag afterwards he might have returned to the office buildings one night and burned the bag in my office. Perhaps yet another of his tricks to try and implicate me.'

'Where are these ashes now?' Royden asked sharply.

'Cleared away, I'm afraid. I told the cleaner to move them out.'

Royden said: 'There might still be traces, having regard to the uninspired methods of some cleaners. I think we'd better have a look right away, Mr. Dale.'

Dale nodded. 'Lee could easily have come back when the place was closed,' he said. 'He had all the necessary keys.'

The Chief-Inspector did not waste any further time. He signalled to Mason, and together they left the office with Dale beside them. The office building was still open when they arrived since it still lacked fifteen minutes to six o'clock. Dale led the way directly to his private office, opened the door and switched on the light.

'Help yourself,' he said quietly, motioning to the grate, then he stood aside to watch.

Royden went to work immediately. He pulled out the rather old-fashioned iron grate completely and poked a pencil amidst the ash, dust, and debris that had escaped clearance. It did not take him long to locate one or two dustings of yellowish, cardboardy stuff which crumbled instantly at a touch. 'We're lucky,' he said curtly. 'Get some of this stuff into an envelope, sergeant, and we'll have it analysed.'

Mason nodded and went to work. Royden straightened up and wiped his hands on the duster that Dale handed to him.

'I'm glad you've found some traces,' Dale said. 'If the stuff's leather, or plastic, or something it ought to be conclusive, oughtn't it?'

'Maybe,' Royden said, thinking. Then he asked the question, 'Whereabouts is the rubbish kept, Mr. Dale?'

'In the coke cellar by the central heating unit. Why?'

'Any chance of the original ashes still being in the bin, or has it been cleared since then?'

'I've no idea. Naturally I don't keep a check on such things. We can have a look if you like.'

Royden nodded promptly and followed Dale's lead out of the office, down the corridor, and finally into the fumy, dirty regions where the central heating furnace was at work. Royden went directly over to the ashbin as Dale motioned to it, then when he arrived he clicked his teeth in annoyance.

'Damn — ! It's been emptied. Well, never mind, we may have enough from your office grate. I was simply thinking that if we had a good supply of the stuff it would make it easier for the forensic department . . .'

Royden's voice had been trailing off, and finally it stopped altogether as something took his attention. Dale watched curiously, then gave a little start to himself as he saw the object of Royden's interest. He was staring at the cracks in the ancient, white-washed wall, staring right at the few pieces of copper and silver which Dale had wedged there, and the remains of the handbag clasp.

In another moment the chief Inspector had tugged them free and stood looking at them in his palm. 'Very interesting,' he murmured. 'Very interesting indeed.' He turned as Mason came into view down the cellar steps. As he came over he said: 'I've got a fair amount of ash, sir, and I've put the grate back. Anything down here?'

'Not in the ash can, I'm afraid, but I've just found this little lot.'

Royden held out his palm and Mason frowned over the fire-blackened relics.

'Look like copper and silver that's been in a fire, sir — And what's this other thing? A clasp of some kind?'

'A handbag clasp unless I miss my guess.'

Dale said: 'It looks as though Lee must have burned the bag in my office — probably to avoid the smell of burning leather being detected in his own home, or anywhere else — but the most probable theory of all was that he did it so *I* might be involved. He couldn't get rid of the handbag clasp and silver and copper by burning so he pushed them in these wall cracks to get rid of them.'

'You seem to have a very clear idea of what he did, sir,' Royden commented, handing the copper, silver, and clasp to Mason as he produced an envelope.

'Seems the only possible assumption,' Dale said. 'I suppose he could have buried them somewhere, but evidently he didn't.'

'Evidently not . . . '

Royden prowled round the cellar for a few moments, examining it from all aspects, then finally he shrugged.

'Well, that seems to be all we can do here, Mr. Dale, and thank you for the cooperation. It was most wise of you, to tell me everything as it really happened.'

Dale said nothing, He could not tell from Royden's expression whether he meant what he said or not.

'We'll get along,' the Chief-Inspector said. 'If anything important develops we'll be in touch with you.'

With that he led the way up the cellar steps with Mason behind him. Once they were back at the Yard, Royden transferred the various 'findings' to the forensic department and then sat down at his desk to figure things out.

'I don't know even now whether we found stuff that Dale intended us to find, or whether Lee really put them there,' he sighed. 'Somehow I certainly didn't believe Dale's story. How did you, feel about it?'

'It didn't ring true — and the bit I least believed was that Dale gave Lee five thousand pounds because he was afraid of him. Dale doesn't strike me as being the type of man to be afraid of *anybody*, much less an insignificant man like Lee.'

'Well,' Royden said, after a long spell of thought, 'there isn't much more we can do for the moment except wait for the forensic report. By then I may have thought of some other way to clear up this mess. As I said before, it's the devil of a tangle!'

* * *

The Chief-Inspector was back on the job early the following morning, and as he had expected, forensic had finished their task and submitted a report. He read it immediately:

For the attention of Chief-Inspector Royden. Analysis of samples submitted. Yellowish ash is undoubtedly leather, which has been subjected to fire. The metal samples are sixpences, shillings and pennies together with a clasp from a handbag or some such article — made originally of nickel steel and plated with chromium.

'Very interesting,' Royden said to himself, then he glanced up as Mason came into the office. He gave a rather guilty start as he saw his superior standing at the desk.

'Sorry, sir. I hadn't realized I was late.'

'You're not. I'm early . . . Here, take a look at this.'

Mason took off his hat and coat and

then complied. He gave a slow smile when he had finished reading.

'Well, that seems to make it conclusive, sir. A *handbag* was burned in Dale's offices, and the unburnable parts were stuck in the cellar wall. Beats me why they weren't buried. They'd never have been found in a million years, and even if they had have been there'd be nothing to suggest them being connected with anything.'

Royden took the report, glanced at it, then put it down on the desk again. There was a faraway look in his eyes.

'I've been thinking,' he said slowly. 'This sudden pointer to Lee being the guilty man seems too obvious somehow. I don't say that Lee *wasn't* guilty, but I'm inclined to question the clues that point towards him. Dale could be equally guilty, but because he's alive and therefore open to indictment he may be using all kinds of tricks to push the blame away from himself.'

'Quite possible,' Mason admitted. 'So?'

'It's clear that if Lee *did* do this handbag-burning act he must have done it in the evening or night sometime after Janice's death — in other words some time after January 10th, and before he died. I wonder if Mrs. Lee would be able to give an account of her husband's movements in the evening and night between January 10th and the day he died?'

'She might perhaps.'

'They lived together — just the two of them — so they'd probably have a close tag on each other's movements. I think we'll go along and see. I want to prove Dale's story to the hilt as far as I can.'

Decision reached, Royden acted, and with him went Mason as usual. To their satisfaction Mrs. Lee was at home, but it was plain from her expression that she was surprised to see them.

'Come in, gentlemen, won't you?' She led the way into the lounge and drew forth chairs. 'Excuse my untidiness: I'm in the midst of cleaning out the kitchen. Now the funeral's behind me I'm making arrangements to leave here.'

'Quite so,' Royden said politely. 'We don't intend to take up much of your time, Mrs. Lee. Just something I wish to ask you.'

'Connected with Janice Elton, I suppose?'

'It may be,' Royden replied guardedly. 'However, here's what I wish to know. Did Mr. Lee go out for any length of time between January 10th and the day he met his death? In the evening, or night, I mean.'

Mrs. Lee pondered. She was not a woman who seemed capable of thinking swiftly.

'No,' she said finally. 'I don't think he did.'

'Forgive me, madam, but I'd like something more positive than that. Are you *sure* he didn't?'

Mrs. Lee seemed finally to make up her mind. 'Yes, I'm sure he didn't. He was, as I've said before, a man who spent most of his time at home. He had very few friends and most of the time when he wasn't at business he was here — especially since Janice Elton died because it was about that time that he got the money for that new house. He spent all his spare moments deciding what and what not to take to the new house. Certainly he was in every evening.'

'And the nights?' Royden persisted. 'What about them?'

'Everything was quite normal as far as I know. I'm perfectly sure he never stirred from his bed during the night. He was a particularly heavy sleeper, and I'm a very light one. I should have known in a moment if he'd moved — even more so if he'd gone out.'

Royden smiled. 'Thank you, Mrs. Lee — thank you very much.'

'May I ask why you want to know what Martin did?'

'You can ask, certainly, but I'm not at liberty to give an answer . . . Right! I'll be on my way, madam.'

Royden did not delay any longer. With Mason he left the house and, as usual, they had an impromptu conference in the car when they reached the next avenue.

'I think,' Royden said, 'that we can accept Mrs. Lee's statement as correct. She's nothing to gain by trying to pull the wool over our eyes — and all of it would seem to place Dale back in line again as a direct suspect. Plainly, if Lee *was* responsible for burning that bag and hiding the coins and so forth, he must have done it when nobody else was in the building — and that's been proven as wrong.' The chief Inspector frowned and beat a fist gently on his knee. 'Just what *is* Dale driving at, I wonder? I can't somehow believe that he murdered Janice, so what else is he trying to conceal? If only he realized how difficult he's making things by behaving in this way!'

Mason was silent, trying to figure some way out of the general puzzle.

'No,' Royden said finally, 'I'm not at all satisfied with Dale's explanations and excuses. We've got to pin him down somehow — pin him to something really concrete before we tackle him again. Let's see now, his latest story is that Lee knocked him out in the compartment and that when he — Dale — came to, Lee had already pitched the girl out of the train.'

'That's it,' Mason agreed. 'And like the rest of the story it creaks somewhere.

With *what* did Lee knock Dale out? Dale seems to be ignorant on that point, and I'm not surprised. Those convenient spanners one reads about aren't very prolific in a train compartment.'

'I'll gamble it's as big a lie as the rest of his efforts,' Royden snorted. 'But there's one way of trying to set about proving it. That suit of Janice's which we've got in the locker ought to show fingerprints. I know cloth isn't ideal for fingerprints, but it *can* be done by special care. And in this case it's going to be. If Lee dumped the girl through the window there ought to be his prints all over her suit, particularly on the knee line of the skirt and the breast line of the jacket where he carried her in his arms. Okay, we'll set about proving it.'

Mason nodded, switched on the ignition, and the return journey was made to the Yard. In a matter of minutes Royden had gathered together the girl's mustard-coloured suit and took it personally to the Fingerprint department. Here he sought out Andrews, the expert in charge.

'Special job for you, Larry,' Royden said. 'I don't even know if it can be done, but I want it if it's at all possible. I think a man carried a girl to a train window and dumped her through it — and this was the suit she was wearing at the time. You'll be able to judge from him carrying her where the prints might be. Any chance of finding some?'

'I'll do my best. Never very easy on material like this, but we'll have a shot.' He inspected the jacket and skirt and then added, 'It'll take a little time. Both of these garments have to be dipped in a five percent solution of silver nitrate and then dried in a darkroom. Can't do it in five minutes.'

'I realize that. How long do you think it will take?'

The technician glanced at his watch. 'I'd say about teatime. Say five o'clock.'

'Fair enough,' Royden agreed — and left it at that.

Thereafter, throughout the day, Royden contented himself — or at any rate occupied himself — with routine matters, just the same as Dale did at his end of the circumstantial seesaw. Dale, in fact, was not at all easy in his mind at the way things were going. He believed he had made the right move when he had called on Royden and blamed Lee, out and out, for the murder of Janice. But now he was not so sure. Where he had hoped the Chief-Inspector would seize on the story as a possible solution to the mystery of Janice's murder — as the Inspector fully believed it was — he had instead raised all kinds of forbidding aspects, and somehow had not seemed convinced in the least.

The only thing to do now, Dale decided, was to sit tight and hope for the best. Things had become too involved now to explain that Janet had really committed suicide, so the best solution was obviously to blame the entire business on a man who wouldn't suffer and couldn't speak . . .

And at the Yard, towards five o'clock Royden got a ring from Dabs to come and have a look at progress to date, and to bring with him the specimen cards containing prints of Lee and Dale.

Royden promptly complied and with Mason and the chief technician he presently found himself studying several photographs on the expert's desk.

'The jacket and skirt dried out all right,' the expert said, 'and left prints which we could photograph by ultra violet light. Here they are. There seem to be two sets, and since it's unlikely the girl's own prints will be involved in a matter like this it struck me that Lee and Dale would be the most possible. Now, let's make a check.'

Royden moved aside and the expert went to work with the tools of his trade, measuring, ruling, calculating. The Chief-Inspector and Mason watched him in silent fascination, duly impressed by this demonstration of meticulous work which was normally out of their department.

'Mmmm,' the technician said finally, straightening up. 'There doesn't seem to be much doubt about it. Here are Dale's prints and Lee's. And here's the corresponding points on the jacket and skirt.'

The expert led the way into a darkroom, closed the doors, and then switched on a ruby light. The girl's jacket and skirt hovered in an abyss supported by clips. The expert moved towards them and tackled the jacket first.

'Here are the points where Dale's prints are visible,' he said, indicating two positions on a line with where the girl's shoulder blades must have been. 'And here are Lee's prints.'

He turned to the skirt and indicated a point at roughly the knee position. Then he came back to Royden's side.

'There are other prints from both men, not as clearly marked,' he said, 'and roughly in the same places as those I've indicated. From the look of things, I'd say that the deeper prints were caused by the men carrying a weight — the girl's body of course. There might be others, but the suit's rather dirty in parts where the girl fell on the railway track and useless as far as prints are concerned.'

'Don't worry about them, Larry,' Royden said quietly. 'I've got all I need. And I might as well take that suit along with me and put it back in the locker.'

'Okay.' The expert took it from the clips and handed it over, then he led the way out to the normal laboratory again.

'Thanks a lot,' Royden said, blinking in the return of white light, and with Mason beside him headed back for his own office. Once there he put the suit back in the locker and then lighted a cigarette.

'Altogether, a very interesting experiment,' he said, and Mason gave a nod.

'Interesting — and significant.'

'Uh-huh. Dale ought to know better than to try conclusions with the forensic department.'

'He probably never gave it a thought, sir. There aren't many people who know that fingerprints can be found on cloth, anyway. So what's the next move? Get Dale to explain himself?'

'If he can!' Royden snapped. 'I'm curious to find out how many more manoeuvres Dale is going to make to avoid telling the truth . . . ' He glanced at the clock. 'He might be in even at this time — it's only half past five. Let's go and see.'

Dale was in, and he looked vaguely uneasy as Royden and Mason came into his office. He could analyse from their expressions that things were anything but going in his favour.

'This is getting to be a habit, gentlemen,' he commented. 'What is on your minds this time?'

'I'll be frank, Mr. Dale,' Royden said, with unusual coldness in his voice. 'I'm getting rather tired of your continual lying. Why don't you tell the truth for a change?'

Dale's bulldog face set. 'What have I done now?'

'First, there's the matter of your rather odd story concerning Lee's return here to burn a handbag. I've checked on that and I'm persuaded that it couldn't have happened.'

Dale felt as though something were clutching at him, even though his face remained expressionless.

'Can I ask who, or what, persuaded you?'

'Yes! I've no objection to your knowing. I had a few words with Mrs. Lee this morning and she doesn't remember any instance when her husband left home once he had arrived there after his day's work. I'm satisfied that she was telling the truth.'

164

Dale shrugged. 'Well, then, that rather upsets calculations, doesn't it? If Lee didn't burn the handbag, who did?'

'Is that so hard to discover?' Royden asked bitterly.

'If you mean me, Inspector, think again. There's another answer. Lee was intimate with quite a few members of my staff: he might even have entrusted the bag to one of them to dispose of.'

The Chief-Inspector shook his head. 'It won't do, Mr. Dale. It won't *do*! No man who's involved in murder would ever trust anybody else to get rid of the evidence for him. Besides, there are other considerations.'

'Such as?'

Royden said: 'You told me that Lee knocked you out on the train, and that when you recovered he told you that he had thrown the girl out of the window — or at any rate had pushed her off the train.'

'That's exactly what happened.'

The rapier eyes sharpened. 'Are you quite sure?'

'Absolutely.' Dale looked impassive but

inwardly his mind was searching for whatever mistakes he might have made. And Royden went on deliberately.

'You didn't touch the girl at all?'

'I'd no reason to.'

'Then how do you explain your fingermarks on the girl's jacket at a line with her shoulder blades — heavy marks too? How is it that Lee's fingerprints, likewise heavy, are on her skirt at the knee level? To say nothing of various other prints not quite so distinct.'

Dale was silent, too startled actually to know what to say.

'You and Lee carried the girl between you,' Royden said. 'That's how those prints got there. Fingerprints don't lie, so there's no use denying your actions.'

8

Dale Disappears

After a long interval Dale spoke. He did so hesitantly, as though he were by no means sure of himself — which he certainly was not.

'I remember now. Those prints must have got on to the girl at first — when Lee showed me her lying on the seat of the compartment. I recall that I lifted her head and shoulders to listen for her heart.'

Royden was silent, wondering how many more contortions Dale was going to go through to evade telling the truth.

'Wouldn't it have been simpler to take the girl's pulse, Mr. Dale?'

'I suppose so, really. I didn't give it much thought. I just listened for her heart and then laid her back on the seat. I'd forgotten all about that when I said I never touched her.'

'Your memory seems rather shaky all through the business, Mr. Dale. You keep leaping off on the most unconvincing subterfuges and don't once give me the real story. You do realize that I'm trying to help you, don't you?'

It was Dale's turn to give a cold smile. 'I wish I could believe that, Inspector. I have never found the police to be philanthropists, exactly. They're poised like tigers, ready to spring the moment they get the chance.'

'And you think I'm that type?'

'All of you are. The law makes you that way.'

'I disagree. There are Inspectors — and Inspectors.'

There was a long silence, then Royden said quietly, 'Then there's nothing more you wish to tell me?'

'I've told you all I can, Inspector. It was Lee who killed Janice, and I've told you how. It is purely circumstantial that I seem to be implicated in it — not a thing you can prove. Now why don't you leave me *alone*?'

'All right.' The Chief-Inspector shrugged

168

and got to his feet. 'I'll do that just for the time being.'

Dale watched them go, then for a while he sat tapping his fingers on the desk and meditating. Things were moving far too swiftly for his liking and he knew perfectly well that he couldn't extricate himself much longer. He could tell the truth, of course, and he bitterly regretted that he had not done so at first. In fact, come to think of it, he would have done so had not Lee interfered with his insidious suggestions. Lee! Lee! If only *he* had not been mixed up in this nightmare business. It would have been easy — or would it? Even as Lee had said, the police perhaps wouldn't accept the view of suicide.

'Too late now to go back on my tracks,' Dale muttered, getting up from the desk and lighting a cigarette. 'Just as I thought before — if I twist things back now to suicide on Janice's part they won't listen. They might have done at first, but not now, after the lies I've told and the efforts I've made to indict Lee. What else is there I could try?'

He stood staring at the desk, dragging

at his cigarette meanwhile. A variety of ideas occurred to him — ideas which might perhaps implicate Martin Lee still further and give Scotland Yard a good deal of work to do, but in the end Dale shook his head.

'Won't do,' he muttered. 'Up to now I've made use of the things that did happen — and a nice fine mess I've got myself into. If I *invent* things that weren't really there heaven knows where I'll be. No . . . it won't do.'

He reflected further and then gave a frown. 'Funny they don't take more action than they do. There can't be much more they need to sort out, surely? Why don't they arrest me on suspicion, then? Or is it that they really think Lee *was* the culprit and are looking for some final thing to satisfy themselves?'

Dale gave this careful thought, then so confused was his mind he arrived at a startling conclusion. Royden had said he'd leave him alone — for the time being. Maybe he intended to try and find further evidence to prove absolutely that Lee had been the culprit, and if he didn't he'd accept the only other conclusion — that Dale was the one. He had the proof already that he had been a helper in carrying the girl to the train window.

'I can't risk it,' Dale muttered to himself. 'He's not going to come here again with his damned questions. I can't stand it . . . Now, let me *think*.'

He did so — hard, and the final conclusion he arrived at was rather panicky to say the least. He'd disappear. Yes, that was it — get away from Royden's perpetual questions. Better to disappear than finally be arrested for a murder, which he hadn't committed.

That was the answer, and such was his state of mind he didn't weigh things up with the cold precision usual to him. It was at dinner that evening when he said casually to his wife:

'I shall have to go away for a few days, my dear. Up to Scotland again. I don't seem to be getting the results I expected from Highland Amalgamated so I'm afraid the only way out is to make personal contact.'

'Yes, dear — Just as you say.'

Dale muttered to himself. Confound it, why the devil did his wife have to sit there so complacently and accept everything? Why didn't she — ? Dale checked himself and gave a bitter smile. That line of reaction wasn't going to get him anywhere. He loved his wife and he had no reason to feel infuriated against her. After all, she was outside his problem — right outside where all the world was lovely and police officers did not exist. Lucky woman! Happy woman!

Dale's thoughts wandered off — back to a railway compartment on the Scots Express. Janice Elton was standing there, with her big black handbag.

'I'm going to leave you something to remember me by, something that will knock you from that high perch you sit on . . . '

Dale pinched finger and thumb to his eyes. By heaven, she'd certainly succeeded!

'Nothing wrong, dear, is there?'

'Eh?' Dale looked up across the table. 'Why no, Ruth. Just a touch of headache, that's all.'

'Headache? That's unusual for you, isn't it?'

'Yes — I suppose it is really. I've had a very harassing day.'

Though he answered quietly enough Dale wished Ruth didn't have to make such a lot of irrelevancies. That was just the trouble. If she'd say yes and no and leave it at that it would make things easier all round.

'When do you propose going away?' she asked presently.

'I'm going tonight, on the ten twenty. I've left everything fixed at the office so the staff will know what to do.'

'I suppose it's harder for you without Lee to help you, isn't it?'

Dale's face became grim. 'I can manage quite well without him, dear, thank you.'

Silence as the meal proceeded, then Ruth asked a question:

'Are you likely to be away long?'

'I've no idea. Depends on how much business I have to attend to. Why?'

'Oh, I just wondered. This might be as good a chance as any to pay Clara a visit.

I promised I would a long time ago, but things have sort of just drifted.'

'I should see her,' Dale said briefly. 'I'll be away several days at least . . . '

'Very well, dear.' Ruth smiled gently. 'I know now what to do — And I'm sorry if I irritate you. I know you must have a lot on your mind.'

'Why should I have?' Dale demanded, instantly suspicious that the worry of Janice Elton was beginning to peep through his reserve.

'Well, you *did* say you'd had a harassing day, didn't you?' Ruth was looking vaguely surprised. 'I suppose you mean because of Highland Amalgamated?'

'Yes — yes, of course. Sorry if I seemed snappy: it wasn't intentional . . . '

'No — of course not. I quite understand, dear.'

Dale sighed gently to himself. Be so much better if his wife didn't always 'quite understand'. The whole business was getting on his nerves, so much so that he realized he had got to terminate this intimacy at the dinner table as quickly as possible before he said something he didn't intend. He reflected for a moment and then said quietly:

'Ruth . . . '

'Yes, dear?'

'It's just possible that while I'm away there may be a call on the 'phone, or a personal visit, from Scotland Yard.'

'Scotland Yard!' Ruth looked up sharply.

'Yes. About the Janice Elton business. I've told you all about it — that the police are investigating the circumstances of her death. They often come to the office for bits of information — and when they find I'm not there they'll presumably come on here. Let them know I'm in Scotland for a few days, won't you?'

'That won't be so easy if I'm visiting Clara.'

'Mmm — I suppose it won't.' Dale pursed his lips. 'I'd forgotten for the moment — All right, never mind. The Yard will draw their own conclusions when they find the house shut up.'

'I can easily give up the idea of going to Clara's if you wish.'

'Lord, no! I wouldn't hear of it

. . . Now do excuse me, dear. I have one or two things to do before I get changed to depart.'

Ruth did not say anything, and Dale left the dining room actively. For a long time Ruth sat staring at her plate, wondering, her feminine instincts aroused. Unexpectedly, Dale had said more than he intended, enough anyway to make Ruth wonder if things were as they seemed to be or whether her husband was deliberately side-stepping the police. She made a mental note to leave Clara for a later date: perhaps, if they turned up, the police would be interesting to talk to.

It was half an hour later when Dale reappeared, his suitcase packed, and his attire that of a man intending to travel. As he came into the lounge he hesitated, feeling around in his mind for what he ought to say. Nobody knew better than he that it was extremely doubtful when he would return.

'A bit early, dear, aren't you?' Ruth asked, looking up. 'I thought you said the ten twenty.'

'I did, but I'm calling at the office first

to check over one or two things.'

'Yes, dear. I understand.'

Dale could not help himself saying: 'Sometimes, my dear, I think it would be better if you didn't!'

Ruth caught the nervous edginess in his tone, but she did not comment upon it.

'I'll look after everything whilst you're away, Morgan. On the domestic side, I mean. If the Scotland Yard men call I'll tell them you're away.'

'And what about Clara?' Dale asked.

'Oh, she isn't all that important. After all, my first duty is to my husband. Don't worry, dear, I'll look after everything.'

'Yes — yes, of course,' Dale said woodenly, and he cursed himself for ever having mentioned Scotland Yard. Now Ruth might find out a good deal more than he wanted her to . . . Still, there was nothing he could do about it, except trust to luck.

He took a rather perfunctory leave of Ruth a few minutes later, went out to his car, and threw his suitcase into it. He knew exactly what he was going to do

— disappear completely, and remain that way until it was safe for him to come 'back to life'. Yet all the time, despite his iron resolve, he had the feeling that he was being a fool — even a coward; but it was too late to turn back now. The plan had to be carried out — and carried out it was.

He drove into the city centre, left his car in the care of a garage, and then proceeded on foot to Euston station. Here he booked a ticket for Glasgow, but he did not board the train. Instead he walked out of the station again, left his empty suitcase in a public convenience, and finally took a bus to the east end of the city centre. Here he alighted and started to walk — and walk, gradually moving into the embrace of the city's less salubrious environs, entirely away from the lights and the life which he had come to regard as his especial privilege as a prosperous city man.

Late in the evening he came across a third-rate tailor's shop in a dingy side street. It was still open — and doing business — even if it was against the law to trade at ten-thirty in the evening. Dale hesitated as he drew nearer the gas-lighted and rather grimy windows — then swallowing his pride he opened the shop door and entered the dingy interior. Suits and overcoats hung around him, some of them new, some of them bearing the obvious look, and smell, of dry cleaning.

'Good evening, sir . . . '

Dale almost jumped in surprise. The proprietor — if such he was — came from the jungle of clothes, a yellow faced and heavily bearded man of plainly Jewish stock. 'Er — I think perhaps you can help me,' Dale said, clearing his throat.

'But of course, sir: that's why I'm here.'

Silence. The man looked at his prospective customer curiously, apprais-ing his well cut clothes and general air of affluence. Hardly the kind of man one expected to see in a second hand clothiers.

'I want you to fit me out and ask no questions,' Dale said brusquely, handing over some money. 'Remember that — no questions. Will that cover . . . your silence?'

The man smiled. 'I haven't seen you this evening, sir. Now might I ask what you want me to do?'

'Find me a cheap suit, hat, overcoat, and shoes — and find me somewhere where I can change. The clothes I've got on I want you to destroy — completely. Understand?'

'Completely, sir. But — '

'Well?' Dale snapped. 'But what?'

'I would like to be assured that I am not aiding a murderer. The police wouldn't treat me kindly if that proved to be the case.'

'I told you, not to ask — ' Dale stopped and then shrugged. 'All right, I'll tell you. You are not aiding a murderer: I just find it necessary to drop out of sight for business reasons, and I've come here to be rid of my identity.'

The other nodded, evidently satisfied. 'How about this suit, sir? And this overcoat to go with it? And perhaps these shoes too . . . '

Altogether, Dale was in the shop half an hour, and he certainly did not look like a business tycoon when he finally emerged into the glimmering gaslight. He had on a navy blue suit of very indifferent colour, a tweed overcoat far too small for him, brogue shoes which were down at the heels, and a cap which had long since lost its normal shape. Thus attired, he slouched down the street and finally ended his journey at a cheap night café. Here he ordered steak and kidney pudding and chips, and sat down at a corner table to eat it, and meditate on what he had done.

Of one thing he was satisfied: he had ditched his identity completely. If Scotland Yard wanted him — if Royden wanted once more to ask awkward questions, he'd be unlucky. The only thing he, Royden, could finally do if Dale remained lost, was bring the case of Janice Elton to a conclusion in the most logical way possible. And his superiors would demand such an action in the end: they wouldn't forever put up with testing this and that lead. And it was this gamble with time that Dale was counting on. Once Royden made a firm decision he couldn't go back on it. Then, and only then, did Dale plan to return to his normal life.

The only thing wrong was that Dale was not an accomplished crook. He was not even a good schemer — apart from his business — and for this very reason his disappearing act was such an obvious one that it could hardly have deceived a child. Even as he sat in the cheap eating house consuming his supper two Yard men in plain clothes were watching him, from the inside of a private car on the other side of the street. Royden had ordered a watch over Dale to be maintained, and that was exactly what had been — and was being — done. Right from the very moment when he had left his home Dale was being watched — and the surveillance continued until towards midnight. After which the Yard men felt reasonably sure that Dale was 'parked' for the night, and they then returned to the Yard.

Royden got their report the following morning when he arrived towards nine o'clock for the usual day's duty. He read the typewritten memo and then gave a wry smile. It had not faded when Sergeant Mason arrived a few minutes later.

'Something happened, sir?' he enquired, hanging up his hat and coat.

'Definitely. Here — read for yourself. Our friend Morgan Dale has deserted the city and taken the life of a vagrant unto himself. He's probably the only vagrant who ever had independent means!'

Mason frowned in bewilderment and then read the report through. When he had finished his frown had deepened and he looked completely bewildered.

'But what do you make of it, sir?' he demanded. 'What on earth does he hope to gain by a stunt like this?'

'Peace, Mason — peace!' Royden said significantly. 'He imagines he's done it all very neatly and that he's now disappeared from the eyes of men. Evidently my questions got a bit too much for him.'

'But he doesn't think he can get away with it, surely? Changing his clothes at Isaac's second hand store, having supper in a broken-down hash house, then finishing up for the night in a cheap rooming house. It's crazy!'

'Certainly it's crazy, but at least he's free of the law — or so he thinks.' Royden pondered for a moment. 'I *could* think that he's run out because he's guilty, but I don't. I still believe him innocent, but holding something back, a something that we must get out of him to complete the whole picture. What is he concealing? That's what we've been trying to find out all along.'

'And we seem to have pushed ourselves further away than ever from getting an answer, sir.'

'Don't be too sure of that. This may turn out to be a very useful move on Dale's part, even though he doesn't intend it that way.'

'How do you mean? You're going to put a stop to his crazy masquerade, aren't you?'

'No . . . ' Royden lighted a cigarette. 'No, I don't think I shall. The man's worked damned hard to eradicate himself, so why should I spoil his fun?'

'Sorry, sir. I don't get the angle.'

'Well, look at it this way. Dale imagines

he's safe now from the police. All right, let him keep on thinking that. There are plenty of good men we can use to persuade him to talk — to unburden himself, if you like. He might do it to a down-and-out, where he wouldn't do it for us.'

'Mmm, doubtful,' Mason sighed. 'He doesn't strike me as being the sort who'll give anything away.'

'There are ways and means,' Royden shrugged. 'Any man's vulnerable if an expert sets to work on him, and I'll have the best man I can think of to do just that. In the meantime we're going to convey the impression that we can't find him. It might be interesting to see what sort of a story he's spun to his wife, so we'll make a call on her. According to this the relief boys are still on Dale's tail, and they'll remain so, so we've no immediate worries about him. Let's be on our way.'

So, towards mid-morning, Ruth Dale had the two visitors of whom her husband had warned her. She preceded both men into the lounge and then looked at them in vague concern.

'As I have already told you, gentlemen, I don't see how I can help you.' She motioned to chairs. 'My husband has gone away to Scotland on business and it's uncertain when he'll be back.'

Royden nodded but did not say anything. Ruth Dale searched his impassive face anxiously.

'Inspector, what is your *real* motive in wanting to see my husband?' she demanded. 'I know it's the case of Janice Elton, but that's all I *do* know. My husband hasn't volunteered any further details. He isn't involved — seriously — in any way?'

'I'm afraid, madam, that I cannot answer that question at this stage,' Royden shrugged. 'It simply happens that all the people with whom Janice Elton had contact prior to her death are useful to us in our enquiry, your husband especially so in the absence of Mr. Lee, who obviously cannot tell us anything.'

'You don't believe my husband is a murderer, surely?' Ruth demanded. 'It's fantastic! He isn't that kind of man.'

Royden smiled faintly. 'I cannot answer

your question, Mrs. Dale. All I can say is that I had hoped to see your husband to confirm one or two points. Since I can't do that I shall have to wait until he returns. You've no idea when that will be?'

'No idea at all. I have already said so.'

Royden hesitated a moment, then, 'There are ways in which you can perhaps help me, Mrs. Dale. I haven't questioned you before because there has been no need, but this seems a good opportunity to rectify the omission.'

'Yes?'

'What were your husband's relations with Janice Elton?'

'As far as I know, purely business. I believe she was a good secretary, but for some reason my husband dismissed her. He was rather vague on that issue when I questioned him.'

'He dismissed her, Mrs. Dale, because she made love to him,' Royden said frankly.

'She did what?' Ruth stared incredulously.

'She made love — and be it said to his credit your husband took an unfavourable view of her advances and for that reason dismissed her. Actually, Mrs. Dale, I haven't really the authority to tell you this about Janice and your husband, but I'm waiving rules on this occasion. I think it only right that you should know your husband is quite loyal to you. Janice's behaviour ended in her getting herself murdered.'

'And you suspect my husband?'

Royden sighed. 'Off the record, Mrs. Dale, I don't. I think he's a victim of circumstances, but in building up the evidence for this case I can't just state what I *think*; I've got to know. In the last analysis I have to present a clear-cut case for the law to work upon, and I can't do that without your husband coming into the open and giving me the facts, no matter how damning they may be for him.'

Ruth Dale was silent for a long time. Then she said quietly,

'I appreciate your taking me so much into your confidence, Inspector. All I can say is that when he returns I'll have a quiet talk with Morgan and get him to unburden himself.'

'That would help a lot,' Royden admitted. 'There is, however, the unfortunate possibility that your husband may not return for a considerable time.'

'Why do you say that?'

'If he believes, as I think he does, that we suspect him of murder he may adopt some subterfuge to keep out of sight. That's a common reaction of a frightened man, and I don't think your husband is any exception to the rule.'

Ruth looked troubled. 'I wish I could understand why he doesn't tell you the real facts. It would make things so much easier all round.'

'Perhaps . . . ' Royden mused. 'Put yourself in your husband's place, Mrs. Dale. He and Mr. Lee were the only two people in the train compartment when Janice Elton met her death. Janice can't speak, and neither can Lee. With them both dead, your husband is the only person who really knows what happened. He evidently is in a position where the truth would make him look guilty — and like most other people he doesn't trust the law to believe the right thing. A pity that is a general fact, for we *are* able to perceive mitigating circumstances in spite of what the general public thinks.'

Ruth Dale reflected through a long interval, then she gave a shrug.

'I can only repeat what I said before, Inspector. The moment Morgan returns I'll see what I can do. He'll be surprised to learn that I know so much, and that may give him the incentive to fill in the details you require.'

9

The Second Bottle

'Don't you think, sir,' Mason said, as he drove back to Whitehall, 'that you told Mrs. Dale rather a lot?'

Royden smiled. 'I suppose I did, but I did it more in the capacity of a private individual than a police Inspector. Sometimes it pays. I did it with a double purpose. For one thing, if Dale *should* change his mind and reappear amongst us his wife may be the one person to make him tell us what we want. On the other hand I think it's only fair that Mrs. Dale should be prepared for Dale's disappearance. We *know* he's disappeared, of course, but she doesn't as yet. A little warning will soften the shock when it comes.'

'Yes, sir,' Mason agreed. 'The 'human touch', as it were.'

'Call it that if you like. It doesn't always

pay to keep to strict regulations. Besides, I want some *action*!' Royden beat his clenched fist gently on his knee. 'The case of Janice Elton is hanging about far too long, and if it goes much further the A.C. will be demanding to know what I'm doing about it. He's even more likely to ask questions because the newspapers aren't being exactly helpful. They're already asking what the law's doing about Janice, and I can't give them any positive answer.'

'You *could* play your hunch, and leave it at that,' Mason suggested.

'How do you mean?'

'You don't really suspect Dale of having committed the murder — so why don't you blame it on Lee and let it go at that? Lee can't do anything about it.'

'If that's your line of least resistance, Mason, you'll be a long time getting promoted. I can't do a thing like that: I've no *proof*. Besides, my hunch might be wrong and if it should come out in the end that Dale is the killer, what then? I'll be back on the beat in double quick time.'

'And we're still not believing in the

possibility of suicide, sir?'

'No,' Royden muttered. 'It doesn't fit somehow, as I said earlier. Besides, why did Lee carry the poison bottle in his pocket if it was suicide?'

Long silence as Mason drove through the traffic; then he asked almost humbly,

'What's next then, sir?'

'I think I'll get Jameson on the job. He's a good policeman and a good actor. Between those two accomplishments he may be able to produce something. I'll have him go to work on Dale. Dale's story we've *got* to have!'

And in the meantime Dale himself was wandering aimlessly in the dock area of London, constantly watched and quite unaware of the fact. His only interest in life was the scrutiny of the morning and evening papers, either bought or in the free library. This new state of existence was something quite novel for him, and but for the worry on his mind he could even have enjoyed it. The rest from the rigors of business life and the exploratory wanderings in an entirely different district stimulated his imagination. Besides, the exercise was helpful. He realized how much keener his appetite was, how much he enjoyed the coarse but wholesome fare dished up in the second-rate cafés he frequented . . .

Then, on the second evening of his self-enforced isolation he saw an announcement in the paper that made him appreciate how good his strategy had been. Or so it appeared: that the whole thing was devised by Inspector Royden, who knew quite well where he was and what he was doing, never occurred to him. Dale read the small column carefully in the café, which he had made his main haunt. Under the title of 'FINANCIER DISAPPEARS' he found the full details of his vanishing act.

It was reported this afternoon that Mr. Morgan Dale, the well-known London financier, had mysteriously disappeared on a business trip to Scotland. Apparently, though he booked a ticket for Glasgow, he never arrived at his destination. The police have been informed and are making inquiries. A spokesman said this afternoon that the police fear some harm may have befallen Mr. Dale, mainly because he is an important witness in the case of Janice Elton, whose murder is still occupying the attention of Scotland Yard's C.I.D.

Dale lowered the paper to the tabletop and smiled to himself. Then he frowned.

'They've been mighty quick on the job,' he muttered. 'Soon found that I took a ticket for Glasgow, anyway . . . '

He ceased muttering to himself, aware that a down-and-out was heading for his table, the only place in the café where there was any room. Finally the 'down-and-out' settled down opposite Dale and rubbed his stubbly chin thoughtfully.

'Anything decent to eat here, guv?' he asked Dale, after a brief study of the tea-stained menu card.

Dale looked at him. Certainly there was nothing in the man's unshaven face and threadbare attire to show that he was Detective-Sergeant Jameson of the C.I.D.

'To eat?' Dale repeated, miles away. 'Er — you might try the steak pudding and chips. Seems about the only thing on the list that's any good.'

Jameson frowned. 'Bit dear, though. I 'aven't got money to chuck around. Things have been 'ard with me lately — very 'ard.'

'I'm sorry,' Dale said, perfunctorily, and picked up his newspaper again. He noticed, however, that ' 'ard' though times might be his unwished-for fellow diner ordered steak pudding and chips just the same, and then started to eat them with all the evidences of extreme hunger.

'Out of work, guv?' Jameson asked presently, busy with his knife and fork.

Dale looked over his newspaper and then nodded.

'Yes, I am. I've got a bit of money saved up so I can keep going for awhile.'

'Uh-huh, I thought you must be out of work by the way you're studying that paper.'

Dale frowned. 'What's that got to do with it?'

'You're studying the 'Sits Vac' column, aren't you?'

'I — er — ' Dale hesitated for a moment, wondering what 'Sits Vac' might apply to. Then he happened to notice 'Situations Vacant' at one side of the newspaper page and the light dawned upon him.

'Yes,' he said, nodding. 'Yes, I'm looking for a job.'

'Shouldn't be 'ard for you to find one, being as you're educated, I mean. Now with me it's different. I never 'ad any education worth while.'

Dale was silent. He didn't know whether to be friendly or not. He had made up his mind long since that friends might be dangerous to his disappearing act. Still, there was no harm in *this* chap, surely? And there was nowhere else to go — except into the drizzly winter's night.

'My age is against me,' Dale said.

'That's the same as they tell *me,* guv. Once you're past forty you've got one foot in the grave — so say the blokes with jobs. They wouldn't be so 'andy at sayin' it if they hadn't got work themselves. Ever stop to think, guv, how cocksure a regular wage makes you feel?'

'Mmmm, I suppose it does,' Dale admitted.

'When you ain't got nothin' you're on the scrap heap. Take it from me — I know.' The 'down-and-out' looked up from his supper with a wealth of meaning in his cadaverous features. 'I usta be a bus driver when I was workin'. A good one I was, too. Seems the hell of a time ago, though. Me name's Jackson, by the way. What's yours?'

'Er — Henderson,' Dale replied, on the spur of the moment.

' 'Enderson, eh? Look, tell me something, guv. Don't you find it lonely looking for work alone? Wouldn't you rather have somebody to share your troubles with?'

Dale did not answer. Jackson looked at him for a moment and then said reflectively:

'Meself, I always find it easier to keep going when you've got somebody to talk to. Y'know the old saying — a trouble shared is a trouble halved. I usta be able to talk things out with my wife — she was a rare one for understandin' . . . '

'She's — dead?' Dale questioned, and the C.I.D. man nodded.

'Yes. Bin dead six months and more. It was on account of that that I lost my job. Had to stay beside her, and the 'bus company took a dim view of my being always away. Funny how tough people are sometimes.'

'Funny — and cruel,' Dale said, with a reminiscence of his own experiences. 'Always out to believe the wrong thing.'

'That's what I say.'

In such a way did Sergeant Jameson begin his endeavours to worm some information out of Dale. He went no further on that particular night: he was far too experienced to precipitate things — but he *did* strike up what seemed to Dale a perfectly natural acquaintanceship, which persisted as day after day went by. The two men constantly saw each other in the café, and Jameson in particular related each time how he had been searching for, and failing to find, work. Dale had a similar hard luck story. He had to pretend that he was seeking employment, if only to lend verisimilitude to the type of character he had created.

And on the fourth night, as once again

they sat in the same café over the same monotonous fare of steak pudding and chips, Jameson decided to go into action. Time was slipping by and he couldn't maintain the existing pretence much longer.

'I'm going to tell you something, guv . . . ' Jameson glanced about him quickly as he ate his supper. 'I think I know you well enough by now to risk it.'

'Tell me something?' Dale glanced in surprise as he chewed the rather tough steak deliberately.

'The reason why I can't get a job. I've got no references.'

'But surely the bus company gave you some? After all, it was only because of your wife that you let them down, wasn't it?'

Jameson grinned a little. 'Not entirely. In fact that bit about the wife doesn't mean a thing. I'm not married. I only used that story until I got to know you better.'

'Oh . . . ' Dale didn't know whether to feel annoyed or flattered.

'Truth is,' Jameson whispered, picking

up the bottle of tomato sauce and unscrewing the lid, 'I'm only just out of prison. *That's* why I haven't got any references, and I'm not likely to have any, either.'

'What were you in for?' Dale asked.

'A robbery that I didn't commit. I got involved somehow and before I knew where I was I — Blast!' Jameson finished in annoyance — with good reason. So intent had he been in confiding his story he had inadvertently shaken the sauce bottle, and the top was nearly off. A smother of red tomato sauce splashed onto his shabby suit and across Dale's cheap pullover and his hands.

'Hell!' Jameson said, in genuine apology. 'I'm sorry about that, guv. Never expected it.'

Dale got up, wiping the stuff away with a paper serviette; then he glanced across at the sign on the wall reading GENT'S TOILET. Jameson caught his glance at the same moment and with a nod to each other they repaired to the washbowl — there was only one — and the paper-towel machine.

Jameson washed first, his jacket on the peg and his shirtsleeves rolled up. It was when he was getting into his jacket again that Dale noticed something, in the act of drying his hands. Unintentionally, Jameson tipped his jacket in taking it from the peg and something dropped from the inner breast pocket — to be instantly retrieved. But not quite quickly enough. The object could have been a driver's license or a train contract — both very unlikely for a man of 'Jackson's' supposed standing. As a matter of fact, neither fitted the bill. The object was a warrant card. Dale had seen a similar one often enough in the past few weeks, in the hands of Inspector Royden.

Even as the fact dawned on him he went on drying his hands and Jameson completed the job of donning his jacket. A warrant card . . . So this supposed out of work has-been with the criminal record was another of the vultures. Dale smiled bitterly to himself as he followed Jackson back to their table in the café.

'Like I was saying . . . ' Jackson continued, and Dale listened in polite and rather frigid interest — a pose which he maintained through the interrupted meal, and beyond it, so much so that 'Jackson' did not put his final probe into operation, resolving instead to wait for a more favourable atmosphere on the morrow.

But that was where he slipped up. On the morrow there was no sign of Dale anywhere — nor were the patrol boys keeping him under observation able to supply any information. Somehow Dale had slipped away in the night hours from his rooming house — and was gone.

Accordingly, by teatime the following day, a very much harassed and stubbly Detective-Sergeant turned up in Royden's office to confess the failure of his mission. Royden listened impassively enough but there was no denying the irritation in his expression.

'So he beat you,' he said finally, his voice heavily sarcastic. 'Douglas Jameson, our most trusted man, finds himself licked by an absolute amateur . . . What the devil were those men on surveillance doing to let him slip away? Looking at dirty postcards?'

'I don't know their part of it, sir, though I know mine,' Jameson sighed. 'I had everything laid on to get some news out of Dale — but it didn't work. He was all right until we went to wash off some tomato sauce in the toilet. I'd accidentally spilled it on both of us. Then — Well, I suppose he saw that warrant card of mine when I dropped it out of my jacket. He must have the eyes of a hawk.'

'Just as you seem to have the brains of an infant!' Royden snapped. 'You drop a warrant card: you bungle things by throwing sauce about — and don't forget *this*: Dale is a keen businessman, and he'd know in an instant what card it was that you'd dropped, no matter how quick you were. He's a man hiding from the police, remember, which made him extra sharp.'

'Yes, I suppose so,' Jameson admitted. 'Anyway, tough though it is on me to have to admit it, those are the facts. I've spent all today searching for him, but it hasn't done me any good.'

'Maybe you need a holiday,' Royden said sourly. 'Perhaps the force is getting under your skin . . . '

Jameson did not say anything. Finally, as he realized nothing more was going to be forthcoming from the Chief-Inspector, he left the office moodily.

'Fathead!' Royden said at last, with unusual bitterness. 'I'd have staked everything on Jameson pulling a perfect job, and yet even he has to let me down. This Janice Elton business is certainly a jinx case. Everything we try and do seems to fall apart in our hands.'

'Certainly does, sir,' Mason agreed, sitting in moody thought at his desk. 'What I can't understand is what the patrol boys were doing to let him — Dale I mean — get away from them.'

'They were probably half asleep . . . ' Royden got up from his desk and began to pace the office impatiently. 'I *could* have them in here and raise hell with them, I suppose, but what good would that do? The hare's vanished and taking the hounds to task would simply be a waste of time. My worry is that the A.C. will suddenly realize that we're not getting any results on the Janice Elton business, and then I'll be in hot water.'

'What do we do about Dale, then?' Mason asked, after a while. 'Circulate his description through the *Gazette* in the hope that some wide awake copper on the beat will see him and pick him up?'

'On what charge?' Royden asked cynically. 'As yet there's nothing legally to stop him doing exactly what he likes, even to disappearing. If he were a genuine murder suspect — which he isn't at the moment — I'd probably be able to nab him in double quick time. As it is . . . We'll have to think of some subterfuge or other.'

And in the meantime, though he did not like his enforced exile one little bit, Morgan Dale was lying low several miles from where he had been originally domiciled. He had found a tiny furnished room, to which he would repair every night for as long as his isolation lasted. In the daytime he would spend the time outside, either in the public library if the weather was inclement, or outside in the recreation grounds if it was fair. So long as he kept out of sight it didn't matter very much what he did. He could keep tabs on everything from the newspapers — and when at last there was news that Royden had decided to call the case closed, or perhaps pin the blame on the dead Martin Lee, there would be an end of this hole-and-corner business. Dale knew exactly what he would do then: he would return and blame his disappearance on overstrain and amnesia.

The biggest shock of the lot had been of course the realization that the police were on to him in spite of all his elaborate precautions. Well, they would never catch him on the hop again: of that he was firmly resolved. He had slipped out of their clutches during the night, and he meant to stay out. So completely was he sure that the law was determined to pin the blame for Janice's death on him he simply could not think round the problem any more. The one dominant thought in his mind was to lie low, and the possibility that this might make things worse for him never seemed to cross his mind.

So, the days began to pass once more. Each day he was out, and each night he returned to his solitary room. As for the papers, there was no news at all. Everything seemed to be at a complete stalemate.

'All right, I can stick it out as long as they can,' Dale murmured to himself, seated in the shabby armchair as he read the evening paper. 'Their need of doing something is far more urgent than mine . . . '

He lowered the paper for a moment and sat thinking. The thought of his wife crossed his mind and he wondered, with regret, just how she was feeling. Pretty distraught, no doubt. He wished there were some way of getting word to her but under the circumstances it was impossible. No; have to sit tight and wait and see what happened. There was no other course.

It was on the third day after Dale's 'getaway' in the night that something happened. Chief-Inspector Royden, planning various schemes in his mind but bringing none of them to fruition, was surprised in mid-morning by a visit from no less a person than Mrs. Martin Lee.

He greeted her cordially enough and drew forth a chair for her.

'You're probably wondering, Inspector, why I've called — so I'll waste no time in coming to the point. If, after you've heard what I have to say, you think me ridiculous I'll go, and not bother you again.'

Royden smiled a little at her matter-of-fact approach to things and then settled in his chair at the other side of the desk. From his own corner, Mason sat watching, under the pretext of sorting papers.

'As you know,' Mrs. Lee proceeded, 'I am intending to leave home shortly: in fact, I was in the midst of my dismantling preparations when you last called upon me . . .'

'I remember,' Royden said politely, meanwhile watching whilst Mrs. Lee rummaged in her handbag.

'In the process of cleaning up, Inspector, I've discovered something. Maybe it doesn't mean a thing, but it did strike me as worth mentioning. In other words — this!'

From her handbag Mrs. Lee finally produced a small oblong cardboard box and placed it on the desk. It had a name in red written across it — SALTS OF LEMON.

'Well?' Royden asked, interested.

'That container is empty,' Mrs. Lee said. 'Beforehand, there used to be a blue bottle of salts inside, but I've never had any reason to use them for over a year. You know how one keeps disinfectants and essences lying about in a home for months and never looks at them? Well now, remembering about poison and Janice Elton, and recalling that a blue bottle is mixed up with her death, and that you think my late husband may have been in some way implicated, I thought I'd better report it. Where did the salts of lemon go? Certainly I never used the stuff.'

'It's certainly an interesting angle,' Royden said quietly, his mind busy on a variety of thoughts. 'And I must commend you, Mrs. Lee, for being so helpful.'

'You think it might be significant in some way?'

Royden smiled. 'Well, that's rather hard to say at the moment. I shall have to think about it.'

'Of course.' Mrs. Lee sat blinking and smiling, as though she expected something else. When it was not forthcoming she gave a little shrug and got to her feet. 'Well, there it is, Inspector. I leave it to you to do exactly what you think necessary.'

Royden saw her to the door, shook hands, and got rid of her as quietly and politely as possible. Then when he had closed the office door he turned to look at Mason — and found the Sergeant not looking particularly interested.

'Think there's anything in it, sir?'

'I don't think: I'm *sure*!' Royden's eyes were quite bright with an inner excitement. 'I've got a new lead to go on, something that may turn out to be really significant . . . Plainly, Lee appropriated a poison bottle and didn't tell his wife about it. I don't think it could have been anybody else for they lived together in the house with nobody else.'

'Well?' The Sergeant was obviously

making an effort to grasp the point. 'Where does that get us?'

Royden went back to his desk and looked at the container pensively. Then he said:

'How's this for an idea? There are two poison bottles in this business, but we've only seen one of them — the one we found on Lee, which to me has always been a puzzle because it had no label on it, even though it had had strychnine inside it. Right! My guess is this . . . ' Royden narrowed his eyes in thought. 'For reasons that we don't know yet, Lee had a stranglehold on Dale — and Dale somehow came into possession of what he thought was the genuine poison bottle, complete with label and so forth. Naturally, he would immediately get rid of it. But the chances are that all he really did was get rid of the salts of lemon bottle out of this cardboard container which Lee somehow foisted upon him. It doesn't bring us any nearer knowing who really killed Janice Elton, but it *does* seem to show that somehow Lee had a grip on Dale — was demanding money, and was perhaps even coming with the *genuine* poison bottle when he met with the accident that killed him.'

'The label from which had been transferred to the bottle which Dale has presumably destroyed?' Mason asked, trying to get things into focus.

'Exactly.'

Mason said: 'It would certainly account for Lee being so sure of himself about money. Naturally, if he was blackmailing Dale he planned to have all he needed.'

'And Dale would never have paid up without good reason,' Royden sighed. 'In finding a possible answer for one phase of this problem we run full tilt into another. Even the possibility that Dale really *did* do it, which accounts for his present disappearance, and the fact that he paid several thousand pounds to Lee without so much as a murmur, as far as we can see anyhow.'

There was silence for a moment; then Mason said: 'On the other hand, Dale might have objected to Lee's blackmailing tactics and told him to go to the devil, which would account for Lee deciding to come to see us with the genuine incriminating bottle — only to lose his life in the very act.'

'Mmm, could be,' Royden admitted, though he seemed to be thinking of something else. Finally he thumped his fist on the desk in exasperation. 'Without Dale making a clean breast of things we still don't know where we are. Everything now depends on getting Dale to confess what he knows.'

'Not much chance of that, is there?' Mason said.

'I wonder?' Royden said slowly, thinking. Suddenly he smiled. 'I've got an idea that might work!' He looked at his Detective-Sergeant. 'What do you think would happen if we arrested his wife?'

'His *wife?*' Mason looked puzzled. 'On what charge, sir?'

'Complicity in connection with the murder of Janice Elton, of course.' As Mason stared at him blankly, Royden added: 'Get me our Press Officer, will you? We're going to have the news of his wife's arrest plastered all over the newspapers!'

*   *   *

Morgan Dale stared at Royden, an expression of sheer incredulity spreading over his face. 'You mean to tell me that my wife's arrest was just a trick? That what was written in the newspapers was a pack of lies?'

Chief-Inspector Royden smiled complacently, and leaned back in his chair. He nodded to Mason, who was sitting alongside him at the small table. The Detective-Sergeant switched off the recording device.

'You got Mr. Dale's statement, Sergeant?' Royden asked.

'Every word, sir. We can have it typed up as a written statement that Mr. Dale can sign.'

'Do that right away,' Royden instructed. 'And whilst you're out, perhaps you can send in Mrs. Dale to us?'

Mason got up, taking the recorder with him.

Across the table, Morgan Dale looked up sharply. 'Ruth? My wife's here?'

Royden smiled faintly. 'She's just outside. She's been observing you, along with other officers, and has heard every word of our interview with you. One way glass can be useful, sometimes.'

A few moments later Ruth Morgan came into the room. She entered half way into the room, and stood looking uncertainly at her husband.

Dale lurched to his feet and rushed over to her. She flung her arms around his neck, and hugged him to her.

After a while she took a step back, but continued to hold Dale's hands as he stood looking at her. 'I had to do it, Morgan, dear,' she explained. 'It was the only way to get you to give yourself up. It was all Chief-Inspector Royden's idea.'

Dale stared bemusedly over his wife's shoulder to where Royden was still seated at the small table in the interrogation room at Scotland Yard.

'Why don't both of you sit down,' he invited, 'and I'll explain everything.'

Wonderingly, Dale took his wife by the elbow and rejoined Royden.

'I always knew you were innocent, dear,' she said, settling into the chair formerly occupied by Detective-Sergeant Mason.

'But the newspaper headlines and reports — the radio and television. They said — ' Dale was still clearly bewildered.

'I 'planted' those fake stories deliberately,' Royden told him frankly, 'after I'd talked to your wife. Once I'd explained to her that we knew you were innocent, she was happy to go along with my little deception.' He gave Ruth Dale an appreciative glance. 'The police are immensely grateful to you, Mrs. Dale.'

Mrs. Dale smiled ruefully. 'Goodness knows what our family and friends will be thinking about me — they'll be assuming that I really was aiding and abetting a murderer!'

'Not for much longer they won't,' Royden assured her. 'A spokesperson will even now be releasing fresh statements to the press and broadcasting media. And later today I'll be speaking to them myself at a televised press conference. Soon the whole country will know the real story — that Janice Elton committed suicide, and that your husband was entirely innocent of her 'murder'.'

Dale furrowed his brow. 'What I don't

understand,' he said, 'is why you simply couldn't have announced that the police considered me to be innocent, and kept my wife out of it?'

'But would you have *believed* that?' Royden smiled. 'You'd already demonstrated your distrust of the police when the unfortunate Jameson tried to approach you in the café.'

Dale laughed. 'You mean the 'tramp' with the sauce bottle? Yes,' he reflected. 'You're right, Chief-Inspector. I wouldn't have believed any police announcements. I'd have thought it was all a trick to lure me into giving myself up.'

'It *was* a trick,' his wife smiled, 'and it *did* bring you back — thank goodness!'

Dale looked at Royden. 'When did you realize that I was innocent?' he asked.

'I was never completely convinced of your guilt from the very outset,' Royden said frankly. 'And whilst your fingerprints were on the poison bottle, they were *not* on its container. That struck me as distinctly odd. I checked with the manufacturer on the container, and they assured me that they always label their poisons — but *always*. And then, when Mrs. Lee turned up with her own empty container, the whole thing suddenly became clear,'

'Mrs. Lee — empty container?' Dale said, puzzled. 'What are you talking about, Inspector?'

Royden quickly outlined the significance of this development. Then he paused and looked at the couple. 'Now, I don't want to alarm you, but I still need a final proof to put before my Assistant Commissioner before this matter can be finally put to rest.'

Dale and his wife looked momentarily anxious. Royden hurried on:

'From what you have already told Detective-Sergeant Mason and myself, I take it that you completely smashed and disposed of that bottle that Martin Lee led you to think was the strychnine poison bottle? Tell me again exactly what you did with it. Omit nothing.'

'I put it on my tool sack and smashed it to powder with a heavy spanner and my jack — then I tipped out the powdered fragments into the pond at Carnforth's Wood.'

Royden leaned forward. 'And what did you do with the tool sack itself?'

'The sack?' Dale looked puzzled. 'I just returned it to my car boot, of course, along with the spanner and the jack.'

Royden's eyes gleamed at this information. 'And your car is where?'

'It should still be in the Central Garage in town where I left it,' Dale said. 'Unless Ruth has — '

His wife shook her head. 'I've never used the car. I've hardly dared to show my face since — '

Dale leaned over and kissed his wife gently. 'I can't begin to apologise enough for what I must have put you through, Ruth. But I'll make it up to you, and — '

'Always provided,' Royden put in, 'we can clear you absolutely. After you've signed the statement that Mason is compiling now, I want you to take me, in a police car, to your garage. We need to recover your car. It's vital that the Yard's forensic experts get busy on your tool sack.'

'But why?' Dale looked his puzzlement.

'Because,' Royden explained, 'tiny fragments of the smashed bottle are bound to still be entangled in the fibres of the sack. With the instruments and reagents our forensic boys have got, it should be possible to prove that the bottle contained only Salts of Lemon, and not strychnine! That will back up your story and clear you completely!'

Dale glanced at his wife, who gave him a relieved look. He turned back to Royden. 'You police boys don't miss a trick, do you?'

'We try not to, sir,' Royden said, smiling.

THE END

Books by John Russell Fearn
in the Linford Mystery Library:

THE TATTOO MURDERS
VISION SINISTER
THE SILVERED CAGE
WITHIN THAT ROOM!
REFLECTED GLORY
THE CRIMSON RAMBLER
SHATTERING GLASS
THE MAN WHO WAS NOT
ROBBERY WITHOUT VIOLENCE
DEADLINE
ACCOUNT SETTLED
STRANGER IN OUR MIDST
WHAT HAPPENED TO HAMMOND?
THE GLOWING MAN
FRAMED IN GUILT
FLASHPOINT
THE MASTER MUST DIE
DEATH IN SILHOUETTE
THE LONELY ASTRONOMER
THY ARM ALONE
MAN IN DUPLICATE
THE RATTENBURY MYSTERY

MIRACLE MAN
THE MULTI-MAN
THE RED INSECTS
THE GOLD OF AKADA
RETURN TO AKADA
GLIMPSE
ENDLESS DAY
THE G-BOMB
A THING OF THE PAST
THE BLACK TERROR
THE SILENT WORLD
DEATH ASKS THE QUESTION
A CASE FOR BRUTUS LLOYD
LONELY ROAD MURDER
THE HAUNTED GALLERY
SPIDER MORGAN'S SECRET
BURY THE HATCHET
EXPERIMENT IN MURDER
MOTIVE FOR MURDER
THE COPPER BULLET
THE MAN WHO STOPPED
THE DUST

NEW CASES FOR
DOCTOR MORELLE

Ernest Dudley

Young heiress Cynthia Mason lives with her violent stepfather, Samuel Kimber, the controller of her fortune — until she marries. So when she becomes engaged to Peter Lorrimer, she fears Kimber's reaction. Peter, due to call and take her away, talks to Kimber in his study. Meanwhile, Cynthia has tiptoed downstairs and gone — she's vanished without trace. Her friend Miss Frayle, secretary to the criminologist Dr. Morelle, tries to find her — and finds herself a target for murder!